Death by Dreidel

by

Susie Black

Holly Swimsuit Mystery

Death by Dreidel

Cover Art by *The Wild Rose Press, Inc.*

The Wild Rose Press, Inc.
PO Box 708
Adams Basin, NY 14410-0708
Visit us at www.thewildrosepress.com

Publishing History
First Edition, 2025
Trade Paperback ISBN 978-1-5092-6068-3
Digital ISBN 978-1-5092-6069-0

Holly Swimsuit Mystery
Published in the United States of America

Dedication

Death by Dreidel is dedicated to Jews around the world who stand up for themselves and have vowed that never again, means never again.

Chapter One

My business partner and BFF, Queenie Levine, and I walked into A Jolt of Java, a coffee house in the California Apparel Mart lobby on Wednesday morning. We headed to the rear of the store to the Yentas' table.

The Yentas, Joan Binder, Hope Greenberg, Queenie Levine, Sonia Wilson, and I have been meeting each workday morning for coffee at the mart location of A Jolt of Java for over two years. The now-daily event started as a once-in-a-while get-together and morphed into the glue binding our group of professional colleagues together.

Before going any further, let me introduce myself and explain my role in this tale. I am Holly Schlivnik, President of Mermaid Swimwear. I live on a houseboat in Marina del Rey with my standard poodle/psychiatrist/sleuthing partner Sigmund Freud Schlivnik, Ph.D.—as in Professional Hound Detective—better known to his legion of fans and friends as Siggie. I tool around town in a bubblegum pink vintage convertible passed down to me from my mother. I am on the sunny side of my thirties, and much to my mother's frustration, still unattached.

We took our seats and Hope handed us each a cup of steaming-hot coffee. The other three Yentas saluted Queenie and me with their coffee cups after Sonia placed the latest edition of the West Coast Apparel News in the center of the table. The boldface two-line headline above the fold read **MERMAID DIVES INTO COMPETITION SWIMWEAR POOL**

Joan tipped her head at the newspaper headline and drilled my BFF and me with one of Ms. Binder's patented razor-sharp zingers. "So, what's the story, Morning Glories?" Joan tapped her index finger into her cleavage, panned the table, and pointed to each of the other Yentas. "We meet here for coffee *every weekday* and yet we learned about *this little tidbit* by *reading it* in today's paper. It just slipped your mind or something?"

Queenie held her hand out like a traffic cop at Times Square during rush hour. "Now, Joanie, don't get your panties all tied into square knots over this. Gary swore us to secrecy until the line was ready for market. We're *officially* launching the new division at the upcoming Competitive Swimwear Market in New York the last week in January."

Gary is Gary Burkett—he is Queenie's and mine partner and head of design and merchandising for all divisions at Mermaid Swimwear.

Sonia pointed to Hope and piped up. "Hey, don't feel bad. We both *work at Mermaid* and were kept in the dark like the rest of the industry."

Joan's jaw dropped. "You're saying you guys had no clue a *whole new division* was being created right under your noses?"

Hope nodded. "Yep."

Sonia pointed to the headline. "This is the first time we learned anything about it."

Joan faced Queenie and me. "Why all the cloak and dagger hush-hush?"

I twisted my fingers like a key locking my lips.

"Loose lips sink ships. Gary is super protective of his design department. He is adamant we don't give the competition any sniff about us entering the market."

Sonia rattled the newspaper and laughed. "I'd say that ship has sailed."

Joan funneled her lips. "Mermaid Swimwear is strictly a fashion house. Are you familiar with the world of competition swimwear? From what I gather, it's a whole different animal."

I pointed to Queenie. "Us? We don't know spit about the category."

Joan's eyes bugged.

Queenie smirked. "Fortunately, Gary is an expert. His first job after graduation from design school was as the ladies' swimwear assistant designer at Rapido. He got promoted to head designer two years later when Hattie O'Neal retired. He was head of ladies' competitive swimwear design for four years."

Hope ran her fingers over the crown of her head. "Rapido is a great company. Why did Gary leave?"

Queenie said, "The design trends of the competition swimwear market changed to include fashion colors and prints, and expanded the silhouette selections from exclusively a racerback to a variety of tank suit bodies. But the CEO, Leni Waxman, wouldn't let Gary make any revisions to Rapido's master design plan."

Sonia stroked her chin. "Makes no sense. You'd think she'd be willing to do anything to maintain her company's market share."

Queenie said, "According to Gary, Leni's position was as the biggest, most powerful vendor in the competitive ladies' swimwear category, Rapido *was the industry trends leader other vendors followed*, not the reverse."

Hope asked, "So, Gary quit over his design differences with Leni?"

Queenie shook her head. "Nope. By that time of the season, no design opportunities were available in the competitive swim industry."

Sonia pursed her lips. "Did Leni turn out to be right?"

I snickered. "Only in her dreams. Rapido's dated, stale collection stood out like a sore thumb compared to the rest of the market."

Hope shuddered. "So, they lost a lot of market share."

Hope looked at me oddly when I said, "As it turned out, it would have been better for Rapido to have lost market share. At the time, Rapido owned the lion's share of floorspace in most of the stores that sold competitive swimwear. In many of Rapido's retail customers' locations, the vendor had a store-within-a-store. Rapido's portion of allotted floor space was huge—in some cases, their styles represented up to thirty percent of the total department stock. The retailers had no choice but to go along with Rapido's design decisions despite any reticence or risk having empty racks. Predictably, the Rapido line proved to be a retail disaster and stores were hung with a huge inventory of unsold suits at the end of the season. Any profits Rapido earned evaporated because Leni had to buy her way out of the mess by giving enormous amounts of markdown money to maintain Rapido's position in the stores."

Hope tapped her index finger to her lower lip. "Leni is no dope. After such a disaster, I bet she gave Gary free rein to make all the changes he wanted to for the next season."

I shrugged. "A logical assumption. Instead, to save face in the market, she blamed the season's disaster on Gary and fired him."

Hope's eyes bugged. "Unreal. Poor Gary. My goodness, was he unemployed long? Being out of market circulation for any time—especially for a designer—is a guaranteed career killer."

Queenie looked at me. "What is it that your Nana used to say…?"

I smiled at the memory. "Sometimes bad things have to happen so better things can come to take their place."

Joan gave me the big eyes. "Meaning?"

"It means if Leni hadn't fired Gary, he wouldn't have gotten into the fashion end of the swimwear business where he became a superstar. Gary interviewed at several of Rapido's competitors but the timing was off and he didn't get any job offers. Stan Herman from Pagoda Swimwear got a tip about Gary's talent from a friend who was a professor at Gary's fashion school. Stan snapped Gary up and after only two seasons, Gary's designs doubled Pagoda's volume and catapulted the line from an also-ran into a major force in the market."

Joan pulled an exquisite gilded invitation hand-written in calligraphy to the swimwear industry Hanukkah party out of her purse. The biggest industry bash of the holiday season was slated for Saturday night in the California Apparel Mart grand ballroom. The event *every industry vendor* clamored an invitation for was to honor Leona "Leni" Waxman as the Woman of the Year by Mount Cedars Hospital for her tireless fundraising efforts. Joan fanned herself with the invitation. "Is *Gary* attending?"

I gave Joan the stink eye. "*Of course. Why wouldn't he?* He's one of the owners of Mermaid Swimwear and represents our company as much as Queenie and I."

Hope fingered the newspaper headline and hiccupped a laugh. "Since the cat is out of the bag now, in case anyone asks, the name of our new line is…?"

Queenie and I chorused as if we'd practiced. "*Gold Medal!*"

I made a ta-da gesture. "Mermaid Swimwear is an industry winner, so *Gold Medal* is the most appropriate name for the new division."

Joan smirked. "Maybe you guys misnamed the new line. Instead of Gold Medal, the more accurate name is Revenge Swimwear…"

Chapter Two

After lunch, Queenie and I sat ensconced in our shared executive office suite reviewing the cut and sold report and in-stock inventory in preparation for our upcoming weekly production meeting when Gary called. Gary didn't say why, but he asked us to come to the design studio as soon as possible.

As we made our way to the design room, Queenie asked, "Any idea why we've been summoned?"

I shrugged. "I dunno. If a print or a sample comes out fantastic Gary can't wait to share it. Or, he's so far ahead, he wants to bump up the line reviews from the end of the week to a sooner date."

Pride and accomplishment swelled in my heart as we walked into the design studio. Hundreds of samples separated by the product line sat packed tight on rolling racks. Line lists and swatch books lay on each work table in front of each product line.

Everything looked all set for our line reviews, but looks can be deceiving. I pointed to the racks of samples. "We're always happy to come down and see how our lines are developing. We're curious. What's so important it can't wait for our line reviews at the end of the week?"

Gary swept an arm around the room. "Every product line is complete except one..." His expression turned grim as he pointed to the *Gold Medal* sample line. Compared to the other product lines, the rack appeared empty. The only things on the rack? Solid black silhouettes served as mock groups. No samples in any prints, and no garments in any other solid colors. A line list lay on the workstation, with no accompanying swatch book. Curious.

Panic squeezed my heart. The corporate line review was scheduled for the *end of this week*. This was a milestone date we were *all* painfully aware of, especially Gary and his team. If you snooze you lose in a seasonal business. A hitch in the giddup, especially *launching a new product line,* could kill it before it is ever shown to a customer. It was impossible to imagine Gary allowing such a calamity to *ever* happen. Nonetheless, the rack was mighty empty. So, where the hell was the line?

Then I relaxed. This, after all, was *Gary*—a fussy perfectionist who wouldn't allow *anything* out of the factory not sewn *exactly* as he designed it. No doubt, he'd been driving the pattern maker and sample sewers to utter distraction by now. Still, you'd think that at least one or two prints would be on the rack only a few days before the line review…

I said, "If you need more time to get the *Gold Medal* line completed, no worries. We can do the line reviews of all the other categories and do the competitive swimwear on its own."

Queenie pointed to the nearly-empty rack "Do you need a lot more time? And will the line be complete in time for the New York market in January? We already scheduled a lot of appointments. It's always better to present samples instead of CADS. Nonetheless, if every single item isn't ready, I'm sure the buyers will understand."

I wrinkled my brow. "That may be true, but as they

say, you only get one first impression. The last thing we need launching a new product line is for the word to get out in the industry that we arrived at the market unprepared." I smiled. "We might be overreacting. You ordered all your supplies well in advance. I realize a few delivery delays are always possible. I'm sure we can run things through a second sample line, if needed, to complete everything in time for the market. Are you far from completion?"

My eyes bugged as Gary blanched and pointed to the nearly empty rack. "As of today, you're looking at it."

Queenie gulped. "Gary, what the hell do you mean? Where are all the prints? Where are all the other solid colors going back to the prints?"

Gary squirmed in his seat. "Not here. Not on the way. Nowhere." He sucked in his cheeks as if he swallowed a sour grapefruit wedge. "Thanks to Leni Waxman."

I narrowed my eyes. "What does she have to do with this?"

Gary pursed his lips. "Mira and I ran into her at Stretch America Textiles and Leni went batshit crazy about us launching a competitive swimwear line. Leni threatened to stop doing business with SAT if Elena Sosa sold to us. Elena made it clear that while Leni's business is important to SAT, no one tells them who they can and cannot sell."

Queenie crossed her arms over her chest. "Well, if that's the case, where the hell is your sample yardage?"

Gary sighed. "When Elena refused to back down, the word on the street is Leni made good on her threats and canceled all her sample and production orders.

Rapido Swimwear is Elena's biggest account and there aren't many vendors in the competitive swimwear category for suppliers to sell to. So, she'd be hard-pressed to stay in business without the Rapido orders. I guess she '*changed her mind*' about selling to us."

I pursed my lips. "In other words, she caved…"

Queenie snarled, "It's bad enough for Elena to allow a customer to dictate how she runs her business, but not to tell you she planned not to ship you is unconscionable. If she told you her decision not to deliver your orders, you could have replaced the goods with those from another supplier."

Gary shook his head. "There are no other suppliers. At least none are willing to work with us. I've contacted all of them—begged, pleaded, even offered to pay higher prices and accept larger minimum orders and still got the hole from the donut for my trouble. Leni has threatened them all with canceling her orders if they do business with us."

Queenie growled, "Isn't that illegal? Restraint of trade or something?"

I shrugged. "Maybe yes, maybe no. But even if it is, go and prove it. Suppliers can cook up a million reasons not to sell to a manufacturer."

I glanced at the design calendar hanging over Gary's desk. "The New York market is the last week in January. I realize the holidays complicate this more, but we can still salvage this debacle if we all hustle." I jutted my chin. "Nobody tells us which business to be in."

Queenie furrowed her brow. "Ya got something in mind?"

I turned to Gary. "You have finished production quality garments in the competitive fabric and swatches of all the prints and lab dips of the solid colors, right?"

Gary nodded and I continued. "We give our Asian-based Private Label suppliers samples of production-quality competitive swimwear garments to knock off the fabric and see which of their available prints are close to the patterns Gary originally selected. We give them a package deal to do both the competitive fabric development and produce the prints, solids, and finished goods. We will end up with much sharper prices, and higher profit margins, and beat Leni at her own game."

Queenie narrowed her eyes. "How can you be certain Leni doesn't do her production at the same Asian suppliers?"

I shook my head. "She is only in one business and has a limited customer base. She'd never meet the minimums Asian suppliers require." I wiggled my brows. "Luckily, thanks to our well-developed Private Label business, we do."

Gary tapped his lower lip. "It just might work and end up turning this mess around and in our favor. We're touting Gold Medal as a *fashion-forward competitive line*. What better way to drive the point home than by using fashion prints in colorways and silhouettes appropriate for the competitive market?"

I said, "It may be our best-selling point." I held out my hands as though a movie director. *"Dive into the competition pool in a stylish and functional suit from the fashion-forward experts."*

Queenie bit her lower lip. "The question is, will we get the sample yardage in time?"

I jutted my jaw. "If the factory wants to continue producing our Private Label programs, they will make it happen."

I waggled my index finger at Gary. "Next time you're in trouble, for crying out loud, don't wait until the eleventh hour to come to your partners for help."

Gary's eyes filled. "I didn't want to let you guys down."

I rolled my eyes. "Bullpucky. We are your *partners*. You win, we win. You lose, we lose. How fast can you get me the samples, color tabs, and pattern swatches to send to Asia?"

Gary flashed the OK sign. "You'll have it all by the end of the day. I'll also cut samples in our tricot if we don't get them back from Asia in time in the real fabric. If need be, we show a swatch of the competitive production-quality goods."

I smiled. "You do your part and leave Asia to me. I give them tons of business already, so we are important to them. They will be delighted to have an additional profit stream. I work with one particular factory who quotes slightly higher prices, but will accept smaller unit production runs and can turn goods much faster than the other Asian factories we use."

Gary gave me a two-fingered salute.

Chapter Three

Since the Hanukkah party would break up quite late, I asked my senior citizen neighbor, Muriel Lobowsky, to take care of Siggie for the night. Of course, she said yes. She's crazy about the pooch. He's the grandson the old gal never had. LOL.

Saturday afternoon I dropped Siggie and his overnight bag off at Muriel's boat four slips down from mine at the end of our gangplank. I handed Muriel Siggie's bag as my boy joyously jumped aboard Muriel's boat and showered her with wet doggie kisses. A pang of jealousy jabbed my heart when he barely turned around as I said goodbye.

A houseboat is a cool place to live. Regrettably, it's not the best place to jump off wearing fancy-schmancy digs and high heels. Buddy LaValle, one of the two men currently in my life, and I were attending the Hanukkah party together. Instead of Buddy picking me up in the Marina, I'm driving to his place in Santa Monica and changing into my party clothes there.

I went back to the houseboat and packed an overnight bag for my make-up, sexy lingerie, and nightie as well as the gorgeous beige raw silk sheath street length dress with three-quarter-length sleeves and a Mandarin collar. Then I packed the perfect shoes: dyed-to-match silk beige pumps—two-inch heels sporting beige fleur d'leis attached to the top of each shoe. The shoes were high enough to make a fashion statement yet low enough to table hop to my heart's content and not fall on my ass. I added a beige beaded evening bag and my nana's beige mesh knit shawl embellished by mother-of-pearl beads, shell appliques, and lace as my wrap, as well as a change of clothes for the morning.

****

The party invitation called for an eight p.m. start time. It was only fifteen miles from Santa Monica to downtown L.A. But if you lived anywhere around the City of Angels and were driving into or out of downtown—seven a.m. or seven p.m.—it didn't matter. You can always count on the eastbound Interstate 10 traffic to be heavy.

An industry-wide party, especially one honoring an individual as powerful and high-profile as Leni Waxman, was the hottest ticket of the season. Nobody in the industry refused the invitation, so the event was sure to garner a full house. The underground parking garage in the Mart only has three levels and would fill up quickly. I didn't relish the concept of hoofing it in heels even for a few blocks from a public parking lot to the mart.

At six p.m. sharp, I did a once-over mirror check in Buddy's bedroom. If I said so myself, I looked pretty darned hot. Ironically, I'd chosen to wear the same outfit for this bash as I wore to the Quinciniero party thrown a few months earlier for the niece of Miguel Martinez, the other man in my life. Hmm. I pushed off the unsettling thought as I draped Nana's shawl over my shoulders and made my way out to the living room.

Buddy stood next to the front door straightening his tie as I walked into the room. He turned to face me and his jaw dropped. I panicked. Was something wrong with my outfit?

I nervously patted the front of the dress. "Is something the matter with my dress? Do you see a stain or you just don't care for the outfit?" Annoyance tap-danced its way over my tummy and I struggled to keep the sharpness out of my tone. "I hope not, because it's too late to go back to my boat to change outfits. We'd never make it to the party on time, so this dress better be okay."

Buddy closed the space between us and folded me into his strong arms. His voice caught as he talked into my hair. "N-not care for it? Good gravy, girl, I *love* it." He held me at arm's length as he devoured every inch of me with hungry eyes "You are simply gorgeous from head to toe." I blushed from my neck to my scalp as he gushed. "A feast for the eyes."

I turned my face up to kiss him when a blast of icy cold air came out of nowhere and chilled me to the bone. I pulled the shawl tighter as two swirls of twin tornados emitting freezing air and spinning counterclockwise whirred beside me. My eyes bugged as they morphed into apparitions, and stood on either side of me. The taller ghost is Buddy's late wife, Marie LaValle. The smaller one is their deceased daughter, Justine.

"It's about damned time." Marie pointed to Buddy and huffed with righteous indignation. "Land sakes alive! Mah man always moved fast as constipation. It was obvious he was sweet on me the way he made goo-goo eyes whenever we got together. Still, I mighta died of old age waitin' for the boy to finally git up the gumption to propose marriage."

I opened my mouth to reply, but the two ghosts

disappeared into thin air as Buddy turned toward the door.

He fingered my shawl and I jumped. "Is your wrap gonna be warm enough? We're still inside and you're already shivering."

The words clogged in my throat, so I just nodded yes.

His concerned eyes searched mine. "Are you all right? You look like you've seen a ghost."

You don't know the half of it, Buddy boy.

Chapter Four

Far be it from me to look a gift horse in the mouth. At primetime Saturday date night plus both local professional basketball and hockey teams were slated to play home games, yet miraculously, the normally congested eastbound I-10 traffic wasn't bumper to bumper. The only explanation? The freeway Goddess took pity and smiled down at us. Forty minutes after leaving Santa Monica we parked in the last available *legal* space in the mart underground parking lot. Buddy grabbed my hand as he took the lead and muscled our way into the packed tight-as-bees-in-a-hive elevator going up to the lobby. We joined the crowd of party-goers who, like us, managed to arrive only fashionably twenty minutes late.

We crossed the ballroom threshold and my eyes popped. The staid, stuffy venue had been transformed into an azure fairyland lit by blue and white twinkling lights entwined with blue and white streamers. A wide array of blue and white balloons in the shape of six-pointed Jewish stars and four-sided dreidels hovered over the room hung from the ceiling suspended by silvery strings. Three rows of blue and white balloons strung together and anchored to the ground by grommets formed an arch over the head table.

Thirty-six round tables each seating eight configured into a semi-circle and faced the head table. A cut crystal vase containing gorgeous bouquets of blue roses and white gladioli had been placed in each table's center. A silver mesh gift bag holding a miniature dreidel and a dozen Hanukkah gelt—flat, circular chocolate candies wrapped in gold foil and markings to resemble coins—sat above each guest's dinner plate.

When my siblings and I were children, our parents hid Hanukkah gelt all over the house and we kids raced around like maniacs to find the coins. Once we found them, we used the candy coins as money to put into the pot when we played the dreidel game.

A gigantic electric menorah featuring blue and white light bulbs in the shape of candles stood in the middle of the room halfway between the head table and the semi-circled guests. A huge aerial photo of the hospital and another one of Leni Waxman wearing a construction safety helmet and holding a shovel hung suspended behind the speaker's dais placed to the right of the head table.

After almost ten minutes of wandering with most of the other attendees in a conga line of lost children searching for our name tags amongst the tables, I spied Queenie. My partner was dressed to the nines in a bright fuchsia street-length halter dress with a deep plunging feather-trimmed neckline and her signature sky-high four-inch stilettos. She stood next to her date, smoking-hot textile industry magnate Ricky Greenblatt, at the entrance to the ballroom diagonally across the room from where we stood.

The din of the white noise of the crowd made speaking in a conversational tone impossible, yet shouting like a longshoreman? Effective, but socially verboten. I crossed my arms and scissored them in the air as if guiding a plane in for a landing and caught Queenie's eye. I tugged on Buddy's jacket cuff and pointed to Queenie. Buddy took my hand and maneuvered us through the gauntlet of guests all trying to get to their respective tables at the same time.

Dressed in an exquisite sand-colored sari trimmed in pearl beaded lace appliques, our cover-up and *Gold Medal* designer, Mira Kumar, and her brother Ravi caught up to us. Mira's triangular face featured a smallish nose set between coal-black eyes and full lips. Wavy black hair pulled back in a low chignon laid against smooth skin the color of lightly toasted almonds. Mira stood an average height, with a curvy figure and generous bust. Tall and handsome Ravi wore a silver silk embroidered Nehru shirt over charcoal gabardine slacks.

Gary and his life partner, Ken were already seated at our table when the six of us arrived. Queenie and I made the introductions and air kisses and handshakes ensued all around.

Queenie turned to Gary. "What time did you get here?"

Gary said, "Around seven o'clock. Kenny was stuck at the studio and met me here later, so we came in separate cars."

Queenie asked, "Was the ballroom open or did you go down to The Showroom bar for a drink?"

"The ballroom had not opened yet. The security guard let me in."

I widened my eyes. "Why not go down to The Showroom for a drink? What in the world did you do all alone in an empty ballroom for such a long time?" I wiggled my fingers. "You can only play so many games on your smartphone."

Gary smiled, "As it turned out, I wasn't alone. And I had the time of my life."

Queenie cocked a curious brow. "Do tell?"

"My twin sister Gale called a few days ago all excited because Charles, her youngest son, graduated from culinary school only a few months ago and recently scored a job as the first assistant to the head chef at *Let's Party!* — the catering company providing our meals tonight. Charlie spoke to the head chef and received permission for me to come back to the commercial kitchen behind the ballroom before the party began. I visited with Charlie for a few minutes and then watched as he and the rest of the catering team swung into action like a well-oiled machine and prepped the meals. Their level of organization to make the presentations come out perfect, for each course to be delivered on time with enough time in between courses, and still appear effortless was impressive. We apparel industry vendors could take a few logistics lessons from the catering people on how to get the most done in the least amount of time. I stayed around a half hour. After I found our table, I relaxed for twenty minutes or so until the ballroom opened and other guests began to arrive."

Ken took an E-cigarette out of the inner pocket of his suit jacket and dangled it unlit from his lips. Ravi pointed to the E-cig. "I've read about those, but I've never seen one up close. Do you just need something in your mouth or do you smoke it?"

Ken took the E-cig out of his lips and laughed. "I am a bit old for a pacifier. Since it only simulates smoking tobacco there is no tobacco, so I don't smoke it. I vape it."

Ravi nodded. "How does it work?"

Ken held the E-cig out in front of him and turned it from side to side. "E-cigarettes come in many shapes and sizes. A lot of them are similar to mine shaped to resemble regular cigarettes. Others are in the shape of cigars or pipes. Some resemble pens, USB sticks, and other everyday items. Most are reusable and come with a power source like a battery, a heating element or atomizer to vaporize the liquid solution, and a place to hold the liquid such as a cartridge or a tank to fill the liquid into. E-cigarettes produce an aerosol by heating a liquid called e-liquid which contains nicotine, as well as flavorings, and other chemicals that help to make the aerosol. Instead of smoke, you inhale the vapor. The e-liquid quickly cools into an aerosol of tiny droplets, vapor, and air. The vapor is mainly made up of propylene glycol glycerin, and nicotine. You activate the E-cig by either taking a puff or pressing a button. You inhale this vaporized aerosol into your lungs. It is the reason using an E-cigarette is called vaping."

Ravi made a take-it-away gesture. "So, are you going to vape here?"

Ken shook his head. "Nope. It's illegal in California to use an E-cig anywhere cigarette smoking is prohibited."

Mira asked, "Do you prefer the E-cig to a regular cigarette?"

Ken said, "No. But it is less harmful than regular cigarettes. That's why I made the switch."

Ravi asked, "You smoked for a long time?"

Ken shook his head. "I never smoked until I enlisted in the Army. Immediately after completing basic training, my unit received orders to go to Afghanistan. Every guy in my unit was scared senseless and smoked to calm down. It didn't take long to get hooked. After I mustered out, I tried everything to quit. *Nothing worked.*" He twisted the E-cig between his index finger and thumb. "At least there is no tobacco using this."

Queenie pointed to a couple seated two tables from ours. "Holy moly. *Of all the people. Allen Brown and Sharon Hancock* are nice and cozy together. Talk about shoving it right up Leni's nose."

My eyes followed her finger. "No kidding." I giggled. "Imagine the fireworks if Leni sees *those two* together...especially at a shindig thrown in *Leni's* honor."

Mira craned her neck. "Who are they?"

I answered, "Allen Brown is the CEO of Winners Circle Swimwear, a direct competitor of Rapido Swimwear. The industry chatter is Allen and Leona have been feuding for years over a fabric that adds speed to a swimmer by repelling water off a swimsuit. Allen says he developed it and Leni stole it. They are in the midst of a bitter lawsuit. So far, the lawsuit isn't going well for Allen and he has been overheard threatening Leni. The woman is Sharon Hancock. She is the ex-Sales VP of Rapido Swimwear. Sharon got fired by Leona after she failed to reach her required volume numbers. Sharon insisted the Rapido product was not in line with the market trends, and is the reason the orders didn't come in."

Queenie dipped her head at Gary. "Another case of history repeats itself. The first time Leni didn't go in the direction the market trended so, her line stunk, and she fired Gary. This time she fired the sales exec. If she wants to play the blame game, Leni ought to look in the mirror. The word on the street is divorced, single parent

Sharon is running out of severance money. She is having a tough time finding another job and accuses Leni of bad-mouthing her in the industry." Queenie clasped her hands together as if in prayer. "Please Goddess above, let Sharon and Allen join forces. Between them and us, we'll kick Leni's ass this season. If ever a woman needed a good dose of humility, Leni Waxman is the one."

Gary pinched his lips into a tight line. "Well, tonight's industry Leni Lovefest won't propel *that* cause forward."

A few minutes later, Queenie, Gary, and I excused ourselves and made our way to the other two tables Mermaid Swimwear purchased for the event to greet our employees and their guests. After chatting with our staff, we stopped for a meet and greet at a table of retailers. The buyers and their management from Allied Stores, Bainbridge Department Store, Carefree Casuals, and Goliath Sporting Goods seemed in a jovial mood. Even Sue Ellen Magee, for her at least, acted happy to see us— or she needed something and used the party hardy persona to butter us up. Geez, when did I become such a cynic?

We finished our schmoozing and I surveyed the room on the way back to our table. The rest of the guests also managed to find their assigned seats as well as the hospital executives and Leni's entourage already seated at the head table.

The only person missing? The guest of honor. Good gravy, did Leni get cold feet? Nah. The concept of powerful, pushy Leni Waxman getting a sudden case of stage fright and relinquishing even a moment of being in the spotlight? Laughable, to say the least. Nonetheless, the crowd turned restless and it begged the question:

Where the hell was Leni?

As if they sensed the crowd's impatience, an army of tuxedo-clad waiters appeared out of nowhere. They fanned out into the room with the precision of a marching band carrying trays of nibble food and bottles of red and white wines to every table.

Twenty minutes later, the buzz of conversation suddenly stopped as the lights flickered. A canned trio of trumpets played a fanfare as the doors to the ballroom swung open. The crowd stood facing the ballroom entrance holding their wine glasses high to toast the arrival of Leona Waxman. Shoulders back, head held high, and decked out in a stunning clingy silver lurex knit street-length long-sleeved dress featuring an asymmetrical faux-button collar and accented by a gorgeous corsage made of a spray of blood-red baby roses, mid-sixtyish, slight, rail-thin Leni finger-combed her wiry corkscrew, silvery-gray hair coiffed in an Afro. She fawned for the press with an imperial wave, then made her grand entrance in a flourish.

The guest of honor surveyed the crowd through piercing emerald eyes as she strode into the ballroom with the arrogant confidence of a conquering general. As she made her way to the head table, Leni stopped briefly at our table and locked eyes with Gary. His cheeks bunched when Leni blew him a kiss. He flinched as she threw her head back and evilly laughed before moving on.

Queenie sat on Gary's left side. She elbowed him in the ribs and jerked her chin toward Leni's receding backside. "What was *that* all about?"

Gary drew his lips into a tight line. "Leni's way of sending me a message."

Gary giggled when Ken asked, "What *kind* of message? Is she one of those cougars?" Ken sucked in his lips as if he'd bitten into a lemon. "For God's sake! She's gotta be at least twenty years your senior if not more, and *she's hitting on you?* Gar baby…seriously…the woman doesn't realize you're *gay?*"

Gary fondly patted Ken's cheek. "*Trust me,* honey. You've *nothing* to worry about. The *only person* Leni Waxman has eyes for is the one she sees in a mirror." Gary pursed his lips. "Leona Waxman is *not* a woman who enjoys competition. Her Modus Operandi is to destroy it. After she fired me, I interviewed with several of Rapido's competitors. I'd become a threat, and she tried her best to tank my career. Once I came over to the fashion side of swimwear, she backed off and I figured I'd seen the last of her shenanigans."

Mira nodded yes when Gary looked over at her. "Do you remember the scene Leni caused when we ran into her a few weeks ago at Stretch America Textiles?" Gary canvassed the table. "Elena Sosa walked us out of her office as Leni came into the building. Leni overheard Elena reconfirm our sample yardage delivery dates and Ms. Waxman threw a tizzy of a fit. She threatened to cancel all her production orders if Elena sold to us. Elena replied she valued Leni's business, but *no one* told her which vendors to sell to, and Leni burst out laughing. Leni spat, '*Get real, sister. Who are you kidding? Rapido Swimwear is your biggest customer. You won't last a season without our business*'. Then she stomped out the door." Gary barked a bitter laugh. "Think that ended it? Think again. Leni was just getting warmed up. She made our Gold Medal line her personal project. She ramped up her attacks by trying to blackball us at every fabric supplier in the industry."

Ricky Greenblatt nodded his agreement. "You ain't whistling Dixie. She called *all* her suppliers, *including me*, spouting some cock and bull story alleging you stole a whole slew of new design ideas from her before you left Rapido and are now using *them* for your new division. And then she gave every supplier an ultimatum. She demanded we all make a choice: either sell her or sell you."

Queenie reminded me of my nana as she tapped her index finger on her nose. "Hol, your nana used to say…?"

The memory of Nana's wit and wisdom melted my heart. "Man plans and God laughs and arrogance will kill you every time."

Queenie smiled sardonically. "And right as rain. If Leni pushes them too far and all her suppliers conclude her volume isn't worth the trouble and dump her, she's gonna be the new, improved version of the emperor who has no clothes."

Ricky flashed a set of blindingly white choppers and grinned at Gary. "You got one big set of cajones, Gary, for showing your face at this shindig."

Queenie and I locked eyes as Gary jutted his jaw. "Leni Waxman is nothing more than a schoolyard bully equipped with boobs instead of balls."

The tense conversation was mercifully interrupted by two waiters who arrived carrying tray loads of Caesar salads and thick slices of fresh Challah bread. Once the waiters distributed the food and refreshed our wine glasses, chatting at the table came to a screeching halt as all eight of us dug in as if the Russians invaded the lobby plotting to confiscate all the food.

Chapter Five

Once the busboys cleared the tables of plates laden with the detritus of brisket, French-cut green beans, and potato latkes, waiters served steaming-hot coffee, and trays of crunchy Mandelbrot—think Italian biscotti with a Jewish twist.

While the crowd enjoyed dessert, Leni made the rounds, glad-handing guests from table to table the same way as a campaigning politician pandering for votes. Queenie nudged me as Leni stopped at Allen Brown's and Sharon Hancock's table, two away from ours.

Leni leaned into Allen close enough to identify his brand of cologne. She smiled evilly and pointed to Sharon. "Allen, did you come to the party with *her* or is this just the poor luck of the seating arrangements?" Leni clucked her tongue. "Between the bad publicity of our lawsuit, we *both know you're going to lose* and your line's poor retail sales performance, *Winner's Circle* accounts are deserting the line left and right." Leni jutted her chin j'accuse style at Sharon. "Don't you have *enough problems* already?"

Leni flashed her used car salesman smile and jabbed the talon-shaped, blood-red manicured nail of her index finger into the small of Allen's chest. "The *last thing* on Earth you need is to add *her* to your list of troubles." Allen's jaw bunched when Leni smirked, "Since my business is *so much bigger* than yours, *Winner's Circle* is not much of a competitor. So, let me give you some friendly advice. If you're considering hiring her—don't. Not only does she bring a ton of baggage—a slew of personal problems continuously interfering with her doing her job— but the sad fact is, she can't sell her way out of a paper bag. Once I dumped her, our sales jumped twenty-two percent the first month her replacement took over the position."

The din of conversation suddenly died and the room went silent as a tomb when Sharon screamed at the top of her lungs. "*You miserable, lying bitch! You're* the one losing accounts by the dozen because of the crap line *you* designed. None of the buyers wanted it, so you intimidated them into writing orders. It's bad enough you fired me, and now you're trying to destroy my reputation."

Leni threw her head back and laughed. "Nice try. You don't need *me* to destroy *your reputation*." Sharon's face turned as purple as an overripe eggplant and the vein in the middle of her forehead pulsed with unbridled fury as Leni spat the words out like watermelon seeds. "*Miss Flash,* you're doing a fine job of destroying it all on your own."

We watched gape-mouthed as Sharon leaped out of her chair, clenched her fists, and lunged at Leni. Drops of spittle flew out from the corners of her mouth when Sharon bared her teeth like a rabid dog. *"Think I'm gonna sit back and let you ruin me? In a pig's eye."* Allen and Martin Decker, the CEO of Clothing Concepts, attempted to get between the two women, but they weren't fast enough. Sharon shoved Leni hard enough to make her stumble backward.

As Sharon wound up baseball pitcher style

preparing to slug Leni in the chops, two burly mart security guards appeared out of nowhere and grabbed Sharon from under the armpits. They sandwiched her between them and stiff-marched her toward the door in a perp walk. As they dragged her kicking and screaming through the ballroom doors, her shrieks reverberated around the packed room and bounced off the walls. Sharon's anguished screech came from the depths of her soul. *"I'll see you dead first!"*

In an attempt to regain both her shaken dignity and control of the evening, Leni declined the help Allen and Martin offered to escort her back to the head table. She flashed a hundred-thousand-watt smile to the crowd and continued to work the tables.

Gary pointed to Elena Sosa from Stretch America Textiles seated five tables from us. "If Leni values her health, she'll pass on harassing Elena."

Mira asked, "Why? If Leni is gutsy enough to pick a public fight with Sharon who is at least six inches taller and twenty years younger, why shy away from going after a petite woman like Elena?"

Gary asked, "You saw all those trophies in Elena's office?"

Mira nodded.

"Any idea what she won them for?"

Mira shook her head.

"Those are trophies Elena won in martial arts competitions. She is one of only a handful of women holding a fourth-degree black belt in Krav Maga, the Israeli self-defense system. Believe me, if Leni hassles her, Elena wouldn't hesitate to kick Leni's ass." Gary grinned. "If I ever got into a tight spot, Elena Sosa is the person I'd want protecting my back."

Queenie pointed to Leni, who exchanged glares with Elena but didn't stop to *chitchat*. Instead, the evening's guest of honor headed to our table. Lucky us.

I deadpanned. "It appears that Leni is familiar with the contents of Elena's trophy case."

Queenie glanced at Gary and smirked. "Are you going to invite tonight's guest of honor to join us for dessert?"

Before Gary replied, Leni sauntered to Gary's side. She smiled, but the smile never reached her eyes. She subconsciously grazed her fingers through her hair and then licked her lips like a cat preparing to devour a mouse. "Gary," she purred, "Lovely of you to come to *my* party." He flinched as she patted his cheek. "Enjoy yourself tonight, darling. It's the last time you will all season." Queenie clamped her fingers around Gary's arm as Leni pointed to Elena. "Better lower your projections because by the time I get through with you, a few hundred yards of sample fabric from that tramp is all you'll get." Leni's eyes bored into Ricky's. "There won't be a supplier in the entire competitive swimwear industry willing to ship you a yard of production fabric." Leni's beautiful eyes turned dark as a moonless night. "No one muscles in on my business and survives…*no one*." And without waiting for Gary's response, Leni turned on her heel and marched back to the head table.

The ballroom lights blinked as Leni slid into her chair. Dr. Seymour Levinson rose from his seat at the head table and walked to the lectern. The tall, fiftyish, bespectacled, circumspect man cleared his throat twice as he tapped his index finger on the microphone to test it. "Good evening, ladies and gentlemen. I'm Seymour Levinson, CEO of Mount Cedars Hospital. Thank you for attending the Swimwear Industry Hanukkah party. In addition to celebrating the first night of the Festival of Lights, we also gather tonight to honor the Mount Cedars Hospital Woman of the Year—swimwear industry icon and CEO of Rapido Swimwear—Leona Waxman, for her tireless fundraising efforts to benefit the new Women's Health wing of our facility. They say a picture is worth a thousand words. So, let me show you everything Ms. Waxman's incredible efforts made possible."

The ballroom lights dimmed as a movie screen came down from the ceiling. Levinson grabbed a clicker from under the lectern and an aerial view of the six-building hospital campus came up on the screen. Next, the new wing's groundbreaking ceremony picturing Leni shoveling the first clod of dirt came into view.

Levinson clicked to the next ten slides—a time-lapse from start to completion—the last one in the grouping a photo featuring Leni cutting the ceremonial ribbon at the opening of the new building. "Four years of construction on the fifteen thousand square foot complex were completed two months ahead of schedule at the end of last month."

Levinson clicked again and a dozen slides of the interior of the completed building lit up the screen. "Singlehandedly, Leona Waxman raised twenty-two million dollars to fund this desperately needed addition to our campus."

Levinson waited until the audience finished applauding and then went on. "Thanks to Leni's efforts, a fifty-bed hospital wing is now open and manned by a staff of three hundred healthcare professionals. Offering four surgery theaters, an on-site lab, a mammogram,

MRI, CAT scan, and X-ray facility, twenty doctors' offices, an on-site daycare center, a medical library, and a complete research center, Mount Cedars Hospital now proudly offers soup to nuts, the highest-quality world-class healthcare for women in our community."

The lights came back on and the screen receded up into the ceiling.

Levinson reached under the podium and set an eight by ten gold plaque on top. He looked out into the audience and beamed a hundred-thousand-watt smile. "It is my great pleasure and privilege to bestow the honor of Mount Cedars Hospital Woman of the Year to Leona Waxman." He held up the plaque and waved Leni to the podium. "Leni, please come over to accept your well-deserved award." As she walked to the podium, Leni unconsciously ran her fingers through her hair. She faced the audience who had risen and given her a standing ovation. She acknowledged the crowd with a well-practiced Miss America wave.

Levinson thrust the plaque into Leni's hands. "Leona Waxman, on behalf of the entire Mount Cedars Hospital staff and the thousands of grateful women our new facility will serve, it is my great pleasure to name you our Woman of the Year. Thank you from the bottom of our hearts for your devotion, generosity, perseverance, and tenacity. You single-handedly turned the dream of this project into a reality."

Levinson hugged Leni fiercely. He made a take-it-away gesture toward the lectern and then took his seat at the head table.

Leni stood behind the podium and graced the crowd with an aw-shucks smile. "Good evening, ladies and gentlemen, and happy Hanukkah to you all." She turned to face Levinson and held the plaque up in the air. "Thank you, Dr. Levinson. I am humbled and honored to be named the Mount Cedars Hospital Woman of the Year."

Leni pivoted to the right and addressed the guests seated at the head table. "I would not be here today if not for my wonderful, supportive family." She waved to a slightly built, gray-haired man around Leni's age. "Thank you, my darling life partner, best friend, confidant, and husband Morty." Leni grinned as Morty gave her a two-fingered salute. "My mother told me to marry a man who makes me laugh every day and after forty-eight years of marriage, you still do."

Gary's jaw dropped when Leni turned a third more to the right and spoke to a young woman and a young man in their early thirties. "Thank you, my dear, precious children, Hadassah and Barry for all your support. You are the lights of my life. My nana once said her children kept her young and made her old at the same time." Leni laughed self-deprecatingly, "I admit that while you were growing up, Nana's theory was spot on. But you both blossomed into wonderful, caring young adults and I could not be prouder."

I leaned over to Gary and gestured to Leni's children. "Do you know them?"

Gary nodded. "Yes. Barry is the oldest. He was a college freshman when I worked for Leni. A good-looking kid. Barry had an engaging personality, yet he gave me the creeps. He exuded all the sincerity of a used car salesman. He reminded me of the TV character Eddie Haskell. Not surprisingly, Barry is now a high-priced corporate attorney at a predator downtown firm."

Gary motioned to the dark-haired young woman—

the spitting image of Leni sporting a beautiful blood-red rose tucked behind her ear. "Ah, Hadassah. OMG! Such a transformation! She morphed from a mousy, shy teenager always intimidated by Leni into such a gorgeous, self-assured woman. The word on the street is that Hadassah finally came into her own and is now an integral part of Leni's business." Gary rolled his eyes. "All that aside, Leni is laying it on thick for the crowd tonight. Trust me, the Waxman family will never be confused with the Cleavers or Waltons."

Mira surveyed the table. "*Hadassah* is an interesting name. What's the origin?"

Queenie said, "Hadassah is a girl's name of Hebrew origin, meaning *Myrtle tree*. Symbolically, the Myrtle tree is associated with peace, love, and prosperity. In the Hebrew Bible, Hadassah is another name for Queen Esther of Persia, one of the true heroines of Jews."

I said, "Hadassah is also the name of a Jewish women's organization. My mother belonged to it when I was a girl."

Leni raked her fingers through her hair before she turned back to face the audience. Then she leaned forward on the podium and addressed the crowd. "Thank you, everyone, for attending tonight's festivities. All the proceeds of the money spent on each table a manufacturer bought for the evening will go toward funding a nurses' lounge in our new building. I also thank every supplier and manufacturer whom I hounded year after year to put their hand deeper into their pocket to make a bigger donation to our cause."

She laughed self-deprecatingly and tapped her index finger to her heart. "You may find this a bit of a surprise—I am quite pushy…" She put her hands out in supplication. "Okay, let's call a spade a spade...my zealousness can be misinterpreted as downright annoying in my efforts to raise the money for this desperately needed project."

The crowd burst out laughing and applauded appreciably.

Leni made a half-bow to the audience. "You all may wonder why in the world would I be so tenacious. The project was certainly a worthy cause all on its own." Leni's voice caught. "A personal ulterior motive kept me pushing as if someone's life depended on it...A long time ago, someone's *life depended on it*. Regrettably, no such facility existed to help her, and that someone died oh so young, way before her time. Fresh out of college and her whole life ahead of her, Uterine Cancer relentlessly advanced day by day and ultimately stole my twin sister Libby's future. An awful death, Uterine Cancer is often undetectable until it is too late. Such was the case with Libby." Leni choked out the words as her eyes filled. "I-imagine the t-torture of w-watching s-someone I-I loved w-with a-all m-my h-heart a-and s-soul s-suffer i-in p-pain, w-wither a-away, a-and n-not b-be a-able t-to d-do a-a t-thing." Leni paused a few beats to regroup. "On her deathbed, I promised Libby I would move Heaven and Earth to find a way to help other women beat the odds." Leni smiled sadly. "I made a promise and I vowed come hell or high water it is one that I would keep."

Love her or loathe her, there were few dry eyes in the place when Leona Waxman jutted her chin at the crowd and said, "When I cut the ribbon at the opening ceremony for the Mount Cedars-Libby Waxman

Women's Health Center, I looked up to Heaven. *'Promise made. Promise fulfilled.'* "

Chapter Six

Leni's shoulders drooped as she briefly faced the menorah as though a curtain fell to indicate the end of Act One in a play. She turned back to face the audience and beamed a beatific smile indicating the beginning of Act Two of her big night.

She pointed to the menorah. "Tonight is the first night of Hanukkah. A little history will illuminate the reason the holiday is also rightfully called the *Festival of Lights*. Way back in 168 B.C., soldiers loyal to King Antiochus IV Epiphanes, who ruled over Judea, another name for the Land of Israel, descended upon Jerusalem, massacring thousands of Jews and desecrating the city's holy Second Temple by erecting an altar to Zeus and sacrificing pigs inside its sacred walls.

"Led by the Jewish priest Mattathias and his five sons, a large-scale rebellion broke out against Antiochus and the Seleucid monarchy. After Mattathias died, his son Judah Maccabee (*'the Hammer'*), took over the helm. Within two years, the Jews successfully drove the Syrians out of Jerusalem. Judah called on his followers to cleanse the Second Temple, rebuild its altar, and light its menorah—the gold candelabrum whose seven branches represented knowledge and creation and meant to be kept burning every night.

"Judah Maccabee and the other Jews who took part in the rededication of the Second Temple witnessed what they believed to be a miracle. While only enough untainted olive oil remained to keep the menorah's candles burning for a single day, the flames continued flickering for eight nights, leaving the Jews enough time to find a fresh supply. This wondrous miracle inspired the Jewish sages to proclaim a yearly eight-day festival. To commemorate this miracle, we light eight candles to symbolize the number of days the Temple lantern blazed."

I leaned over to Buddy. "Compared to other Jewish holidays, Hanukkah is a relatively minor one." I joked. "I'm pretty sure the only reason it got elevated in importance is to level the playing field for whiny Jewish kids at Christmas time so we'd quit complaining how our Gentile friends received a bunch of great gifts and we got the hole from the bagel."

Buddy widened his eyes. "So, you got *gifts*?"

I nodded. "Yeah. Eight. One per night for each day of the holiday. The first four nights were fantastic gifts, but the next four the gifts got progressively less and less exciting. By the last night? A pack of bubblegum." I laughed. "One year, I suggested my parents consolidate and give us four really super gifts the first four nights and nothing the last four nights." I batted my eyes. "For some reason, Mom didn't cotton to my suggestion at all."

Leni pointed to the larger candle in the middle of the menorah. "The ninth candle, the shamash, is a helper used to light the others. Families light one candle on the first day, two on the second, and so on, each evening after sundown during the eight days of Hanukkah while reciting a prayer."

I pointed to the ballroom decorations. "We decorated our house with blue and white lights on the outside, and in addition to the wax candle menorah, my parents lit a small electric menorah in our living room window."

Leni held a clicker and turned to the menorah. "Now I will light the first candle and recite the prayer. *Baruch atah Adonai Eloheinu Melech ha-olam, asher kid'shanu b-mitzvotav, v-tzivanu l'hadlik ner shel Hanukkah*."

I stared at Buddy in amazement as he chanted the Hanukkah prayer in perfectly pronounced Hebrew along with Leni.

Leni smiled at the audience. "For those who don't speak Hebrew, the prayer says Blessed are you, Our God, Ruler of the Universe, who makes us holy through Your commandments and commands us to light the Hanukkah lights."

Buddy made a ta-da motion. "Hallelujah! After all these years, *now* I *finally* get it…" Buddy squeezed his eyes closed in concentration. "Only it doesn't make any sense…"

I gave him the big eyes. *"What do you now finally get?* And what doesn't make any sense?"

Buddy pointed to the menorah. "What the funny-sounding words my Mee-maw chanted meant as she lit the candles on a candelabra thing similar to the big one here tonight. When I was a boy, I asked her the meaning of the words. She said she didn't know, but her mother and her mother's mother both did the same thing. Yet none of them knew the meanings or why they lit the candles for eight nights or said those strange-sounding words either." He rubbed his chin. "Why in the world would Mee-maw and her kin before her light candles and say some mumbo-jumbo words in a language they didn't understand?"

Whoa.

Before I responded in a way he would never expect, the first candle flickered on and blazed brightly. Leni proclaimed, "Happy Hanukkah, everyone!" She grinned. "What kind of Hanukkah party would this be without a dreidel? I'd say not much of one."

Leni pointed to a gorgeous teak dreidel hand decorated by jewel-encrusted Hebrew letters inlaid into each side that rested on a table in front of the menorah. "This spinning top is called a dreidel." Leni smiled and clutched the dreidel to her heart. "This one is a family heirloom and has been passed down from mother to the oldest daughter when she reached her thirtieth birthday for five generations. In keeping with our family tradition, I passed this dreidel down to my daughter." Leni pointed to Hadassah and blew her a kiss. "Thank you, my sweet girl, for bringing our dreidel to tonight's party. It means the world to me to celebrate Hanukkah by sharing our family's treasured heirloom with friends and colleagues."

Leni twirled the dreidel around. "The dreidel or *sevivon* is the most famous custom associated with Hanukkah. It is said Jews played with this toy to fool the Greeks if they were caught studying the outlawed Torah. The dreidel game represents an irony of Jewish history. To celebrate the holiday of Hanukkah, which commemorates our victory *over cultural assimilation*, we play the dreidel game, which is an excellent example of cultural assimilation!" Leni shrugged and held out her hands in supplication. "Of course, there is a world of difference between imitating non-Jewish games and worshiping idols, yet the irony remains nonetheless."

Leni traced her fingertips over the jeweled symbols. "The Hebrew letters *nun, gimmel, hey, and shin,* appear on the dreidel and stand for *nes gadol haya sham*—which means "a great miracle happened." She clapped. "Okay, folks, open the silver bag set above your plate and take out the dreidel and the Hanukkah gelt coins."

Buddy took the dreidel out of his bag and turned it all around. "Mee-maw has one of these spinning tops, but fancier. It was passed down to her from her mother's mother, and hers before." He pointed to the Hebrew letters. "Hers is made of mahogany and it is so old the gold inlaid letters are almost worn off." My jaw dropped when he pointed to each letter and said, "Mee-maw taught us the way to play a betting game using the top. You put coins in the center of the table and each player spun the top. How you fared depended on which of the letters on your spin faced up."

Good gravy. If I didn't know better, I'd swear Buddy's family was Jewish.

Leni stood in front of the dreidel and went into more detail about the spinning top. "Depending on which letter on the dreidel your spin lands on face up determines the outcome of the game." Leni lifted the dreidel by the top using both hands chest high and twisted it a quarter turn for each letter. She rubbed her fingers over the letter that symbolized N-U-N. "If your spin lands on this, you do nothing, and the next player on your left takes their turn." Next, she rubbed her fingers over the letter symbolizing G-I-M-M-E-L "If your spin lands on this letter, good news! You take all the tokens in the pot." She turned the dreidel again and rubbed her fingers on the letter symbolizing H-E-Y. "If your spin lands on this one, you take half the tokens in the pot." She turned the dreidel a final quarter turn. "If your spin lands on the letter S-H-I-N, you put one more token in the pot. We will be using the Hanukkah gelt in your silver bags as our tokens tonight."

Leni's eyes twinkled as she smiled. She wrapped her arms around the dreidel and hugged it to her chest. She said, "Whenever I see a dreidel, my sister Libby comes to mind. Hanukkah was our favorite holiday and we loved to play the dreidel game." She brushed her lips against the dreidel and spun it around. It stopped at the letter G-I-M-M-E-L and Leni squealed with delight. She raked her fingers across her scalp. "Okay, everyone. I took the first spin in our game. Now all of you start spinning!"

Chapter Seven

Half an hour later, no one was more stunned than me to watch Buddy step up to the dais to claim his prize for winning the dreidel contest. A sheen of perspiration coated Leni's forehead and dotted her upper lip as she ran her fingers through her hair. Leni drew in rapid, heavy breaths as though she couldn't get enough air. She closed her eyes, massaged her temples, and staggered like a dizzy drunken sailor for a half-dozen steps.

Then she tried to hand Buddy an envelope containing a one-hundred-dollar gift certificate to Bainbridge Department Stores. It didn't go well. Her olive complexion took on a pale, translucent tone. She picked up the envelope with a shaky hand but dropped it on the dais. A deep red blush of embarrassment rose from her neck to her hairline. Her twitching fingers failed to pick the envelope back up. Leni gave him a grateful look and congratulated Buddy with a wan smile when he took pity on her and picked the envelope off the dais.

I leaned over to Queenie and pointed to Leni. "Take a gander at Leni. Something's wrong with her."

Queenie followed my index finger with her eyes. "Yeah, she's white as a ghost and perspiring."

Mira waved around the room. "Because of the size of the crowd, the air conditioning has been on all night. It's not the least bit stuffy in here."

Gary snapped, "Maybe the old broad is nervous."

Buddy took his seat and pointed to Leni. "No question about it. Something is wrong with that woman."

Mira shrugged. "Or perhaps the emotion of sharing the loss of her sister took its toll and she's not feeling well."

Gary clucked his tongue. "Don't let her fool you with her sad story about her sister. I wouldn't be surprised if she made the whole thing up to add some dramatic context to her acceptance speech. Leni Waxman has a heart of stone and only ice water runs in her veins. She is incapable of loving *anybody* but herself." Gary rolled his eyes. "She's probably going through menopause and having one helluva hot flash."

Seeming to rally after taking several restorative gulps of water, Leni tottered on unsteady feet over to a large glass-topped table piled high with door prizes. She pointed to the stack and said in a remarkably normal voice, "Okay, folks the last thing on our party agenda is the auction of these wonderful door prizes donated by all you generous vendors. Dig down deep in your pockets and let's see some high bids. The proceeds are going to buy a library of books for the daycare center in the new hospital wing."

She leaned over to pick up the first item, but it slipped through her fingers. Leni bolted straight up and stumbled as she clutched her midsection and let out a blood-curdling scream. She gagged and vomited down the front of her dress. Leni fell forward and collapsed onto the table. The stunned crowd went as silent as a cemetery when the glass top shattered and the door prizes scattered across the ballroom floor.

Hadassah Waxman jumped up and screamed, "*Oh My God, No!*" Morty and Barry rushed to Leni, but

Doctor Levinson pushed them away. Levinson yelled, "Somebody call nine-one-one!" Then he sprang into action. He carefully pulled Leni out of the glass shards and laid her stiff-as-a-board body on her back. He held his palm over her mouth. She wasn't breathing. He pressed his thumb first on the inside of her wrist and then on the bottom of her throat, but detected no pulse. He put his ear to Leni's chest but didn't hear a heartbeat. He commenced CPR, but she failed to respond.

Ten minutes later two paramedics, pushing a stretcher loaded with life-saving gear and accompanied by a pair of LAPD uniforms, rushed into the ballroom. The hushed crowd held their breath as the medical first responders reached Levinson still working desperately to revive Leni. The two pulled resuscitation equipment out and prepared to work on the supine guest of honor. The doctor's shoulders slumped with defeat. Levinson's eyes filled and his voice cracked as he waved the two off. "It's too late. She's gone."

Hadassah let out an anguished cry of despair and collapsed to the floor.

Naturally, I burst out laughing.

Let's just say genetics are not all they are cracked up to be, and leave it there…

A shaken and disheveled Dr. Levinson returned to the dais. To steady himself, he curled his fingers around the lectern and held on for dear life in a white-knuckled death grip. The crowd gasped as he cleared his throat and solemnly announced, "Ladies and gentlemen, it is with profound sadness I must announce Leona Waxman has expired. At this time, the cause of death is undetermined. The police requested no one leave until granted permission."

The older cop pulled a cell phone out of the right side of his shirt and made two brief calls.

I surveyed the table. "Better get comfy. It's gonna be a long night."

Chapter Eight

Twenty minutes later the ballroom doors opened and Assistant Los Angeles County Coroner Sophie Cutler, along with the coroner and CSI teams arrived carrying a gurney and a large assortment of crime scene paraphernalia. The motley group danced their way into the festivities in the corpse-cutter conga line that had become all too familiar.

With Doctor Cutler leading the parade, the celebratory evening morphed into a case of Old Home Week. Tall, rail-thin, blonde, blue-eyed, nerdy, and brilliant Sophie Cutler and I have been friends ever since fate brought us together as lab partners in Mr. Hepburn's junior high school biology class. The concept of dissecting a frog made me queasy and Sophie proved incapable of writing a decent essay if her life depended on it. So, we struck a win-win deal. I wrote her essay papers and she dissected my frog. It's how she got Snip as a nickname.

My eyes bugged at the sight of LAPD Homicide Detective Josiah Jones anchoring the tail end of the procession. The cop and I go back a couple of years. Detective Jones and I first met during his investigation of one-time Mermaid Swimwear CEO Butch Oldham's murder. The detective and I tangled after he mistakenly arrested Queenie Levine for the crime. Jones and I had a rollercoaster-worthy bumpy relationship. For some inexplicable reason, he didn't cotton to my interfering in his investigation or telling him how to do his job. I solved the case and captured the killer, yet the detective still didn't do the happy dance. Go figure.

Tall and powerfully built like a freight train disguised as a linebacker, Detective Josiah Jones allowed the hint of a smile to quirk the corners of his lips as he surveyed the room and recognized Queenie and me. Jones walked to our table, nodded hello to Queenie, and offered me his baseball mitt-sized right hand. "Nice to see you again, Ms. Schlivnik. I always figured our paths would cross another time." He grinned elfishly. "Considering your reputation for discovering bodies, it's a miracle it took so long."

I held out my hands in supplication and laughed. "What can I say? It's a gift." I batted my eyes. "Detective Jones, while it's nice seeing you again too, respectfully, *why are you here*? Nobody *murdered* Leni Waxman. She *became sick* at the party and *died*."

Jones replied, "The uniform who called the incident in stated the victim's cause of death had not been determined. The doctor also said the victim's symptoms and paralysis made the circumstances of the death questionable. This might be a case of someone falling ill and dying, or it may end up that the victim got some help on her journey to the Lord. At this stage of the investigation, we don't have enough information to make the call." He pointed to Doctor Levinson. "I'd better get over to the body for a lay of the land." He winked. "I hope you aren't offended, Ms. Schlivnik, but as nice as it's been chatting with you, I hope we don't run into one another on an *official basis ever again*."

I smiled. "No offense taken, Detective. And, for

what it's worth, I feel the same way about you."

Jones lumbered across the room to Doctor Levinson, who stood next to Leni's body where one of the paramedics had covered her with a sheet.

On her way to confer with Jones and Levinson, Sophie stopped at our table and bent in half to hug me. The foot-taller-Sophie Cutler motioned to Leni's covered body lying motionless on the floor. "Why am I not surprised to find you in the thick of this?"

Regrettably, this was not my first rodeo. It has been my misfortune to discover several corpses. As a result, lucky me. I acquired the nickname *Triple M* from the cops…as in the *Mart Murder Magnet*. Merde.

Snip wrinkled her nose. "So, Madame Triple M, I suppose you discovered the body?"

I rolled my eyes. "Not this time, Doctor Death. For once, I was just a party guest where, unfortunately, in the middle of the festivities, the guest of honor bought the farm."

She smirked. "So, you laughed?"

No sense denying it. We've been friends far too long. I stuck out my tongue. "You need to ask?"

Snip finger-waved an I'm-on-my-way message to Detective Jones standing beside Leni's body. Snip tapped my shoulder. "My patient and the detective are waiting. I'll catch you later. Try to stay out of trouble for a change." I gave her the middle finger salute as she hefted her medical bag and made her way across the room to Jones.

Ten minutes later, Jones completed his conference with Snip and Levinson. The din of the crowd evaporated as the detective ambled up to the dais and tapped the microphone.

A collective gasp rose from the guests as he introduced himself. "Ladies and gentlemen, I am *LAPD Homicide Detective* Josiah Jones." He held out his hands palms up to settle the group down. "Do not draw any conclusions from my being a *homicide detective*. At this stage of the investigation, the cause of Ms. Waxman's demise is not official. Only after a thorough investigation by the Medical Examiner will we know for sure what killed Ms. Waxman and whether she died from organic symptoms or if foul play was involved."

The guests chorused a universal groan when Jones announced, "The police need to interview *everyone* in attendance here tonight. This includes the busboys, cooks, guests, and waitstaff." The detective waved for quiet. "However, it is obvious there are too many people to interview *all tonight*." We request no one leave the room until the officer seated at the back table has received each of your contact information and scheduled a date and time for you to meet with an LAPD officer to take your statement."

Jones motioned to the younger of the two uniformed officers who moved a table adjacent to the closed ballroom doors and sat behind the table. After he removed a small notebook and a pen from his shirt breast pocket the cop nodded his readiness to Jones.

Jones acknowledged the uniform and instructed the crowd. "Starting with the row of tables closest to the head table, please form a line one table at a time in front of the officer. You are admonished not to discuss the details surrounding Ms. Waxman's demise amongst yourselves here tonight or later with family, friends, and professional colleagues. Once you provide the officer with your contact information and schedule a meeting, you are free to leave."

Jones pivoted to his right a quarter turn and faced the head table. "The officer seated at the head table will be interviewing the busboys, cooks, and waitstaff. Please give your complete cooperation to the police and comply with all of their requests. We appreciate your patience, understanding, and cooperation during this most challenging turn of events."

Without uttering another word nor offering an opportunity for questions from the crowd, Jones strode purposely back to Sophie Cutler and Dr. Levinson.

Wow.

This turned out to be one heck of a party.

As my wise nana always said, things never turn out the way you think they will.

I had no idea how prophetic Nana would turn out to be.

Chapter Nine

Christmas Eve

I settled Siggie in at Muriel's for the night and then returned to the houseboat. I checked the time. Six o'clock on the nose. Crap on a crumpet. Miguel Martinez is the most punctual man I ever dated. And my preparation progress? Regrettably, far from ready for him to pick me up in an hour and a half for an evening at his parents' house to celebrate Nochebuena.

As Miguel explained the event, Nochebuena, literally translated as "good night," means Christmas Eve in Spanish. On this day, many Hispanic families attend midnight mass together, followed by a family dinner. Nochebuena sees one final posada followed by midnight mass, and the evening culminating with a celebratory family meal. Midnight mass on Christmas Eve is also called La Misa del Gallo (or Misa de Gallo), which means Rooster Mass in English.

The highlight of Nochebuena consists of a large and lengthy evening meal with the family. Food could include tamales, buñuelos, cod, and turkey. At the end of the meal, typical Christmas sweets are served including turrón, marzipan, and polvorones, among many other traditional holiday dessert treats. Christmas presents are usually opened at the stroke of midnight. The rest of Christmas Day is quiet as families recuperate from the festivities of the night before, often eating leftovers from the midnight dinner.

In deference to me, the family rearranged the timing of their celebration. They attended an evening mass and we would eat our meal several hours earlier than traditional.

I never participated in a Nochebuena celebration before. The dress code? A mystery. So, I called Miguel's older sister Adela for fashion advice. Adela helped me select the perfect outfit for her daughter Isabella's Quinceanera party, so I trusted her judgment completely. She suggested something in a festive sparkle, in holiday colors with a bit of sass.

A week before the celebration, I returned to Elegance, the same shop in the new section of jobbers who specialize in dressy clothes on Los Angeles Street, southeast of the mart, where I bought my outfit for Isabella's party. I found an adorable street-length, long-sleeved, V-neck dress in a clingy red Lurex metallic with gold Lurex thread woven into the knit. I paired the dress with two-inch-heeled gold lamé shoes and a gold lamé` shawl. For giggles and squeaks, I splurged and treated myself to a sexy red bra and matching silk undies.

After a quick shower, I slipped on the new undies, shrugged into a comfy terry bathrobe, and laid out my ensemble on the bed. I turned on the TV to watch the Hollywood Star Parade while I put my make-up on and fussed with my hair. The Hollywood Star Parade is not nearly as famous as the New Year's Day Rose Parade, yet with its featured cast of movie stars, area high school marching bands, and goofy holiday-themed floats, it is a beloved local favorite event I never miss watching.

Just as I set all my cosmetics on the make-up vanity table and illuminated the mirror lights suddenly the temperature on the boat dropped fifty degrees. Two spinning whirls of freezing air, spun counterclockwise as twin tornados and swirled down, one on each side of me. Goddess above, please save me. I already had enough stress on my plate dealing with this important party. A pair of pain-in-the-patootie apparitions to add more stress to my angst was the last thing I needed.

Marie LaValle and her daughter Justine blew two blasts of cold air toward my face as they chorused "Merry Christmas!"

I brushed a sparkly gold eye shadow across my eyelids and hoped they'd get the hint and go away if I ignored them. Then Nana's disapproving voice spoke inside my head reminding me I wasn't raised in a barn. So, to shut her up, I half-heartedly mumbled back, "Merry Christmas to you."

Justine looked around. "Where's the big doggie?"

I said, "He's out for the evening."

"Is he goin' to a Christmas party?"

"No, however, I am, and since I am getting home late, I asked a friend to watch him tonight."

I had to hustle my bustle to be ready on time and answering questions only put me further behind schedule. A rousing rendition of *Joy to the World* blared from the TV and gave me the solution to my problem.

I asked her, "Do you enjoy parades?"

Justine clapped and jumped up and down. "Yes, ma'am, I do!"

I pointed to the TV. "Okay, then sit down in front of the TV and watch the Hollywood Star Christmas Parade."

"Will Santa Claus be in the parade?"

I nodded. "Yes, indeed he will. His float will be the

last one in the parade."

She giggled with delight and sat cross-legged in front of the TV.

Marie's ears perked up at the word *party*. She glanced at my bathrobe. "You best shake a leg, girlie. Mah Cajun boy don't fancy bein' kept waitin'." She floated over to my bed and fingered my ensemble. I shivered as Marie's fingers coated the dress with icicles. She gave a loud wolf whistle and whooped, "Honey chile, after mah Buddy gets a gander of you in this here smokin' hot dress, it's gonna be all over but the shoutin'." She tapped the bed and cackled, "You better plan on bein' late to the party. You might not ever make it out of this here boat altogether."

And now for the fun part of this delightful conversation. Only if an appendectomy is your idea of a rip-snorting good time. "I'm going to the party with somebody else tonight, so Buddy will see my dress another time."

Marie's back stiffened. "Who else *except* mah Cajun boy could you *possibly* be goin' *anywhere* with?"

I brushed my upper eyelashes with a stroke of mascara and sniffed, "It's none of your business who I spend my time with."

Marie blew a puff of freezing air in my face. "Well, I'm *makin' it my business*, girlie! You and mah Cajun boy are *destined* to be together, so you better git with the program and fast."

As my face defrosted, I almost put my eye out with the mascara wand when Justine, quietly watching the parade, suddenly pointed to the TV and screamed, pardon the pun, loud enough to wake the dead. *"Mama! Look at the lady wearing a Santa Claus costume in the*

*parade! She just jumped onto the float with Santa sittin'
in his sleigh and took her red jacket off. Mama, she's not
wearin' anythin' under her jacket. The lady has blinkin'
Christmas lights hangin' off her ta-ta's, and they're
playin' Daddy's favorite Christmas carol."*

Marie and I grinned at one another. Marie chuckled
sardonically. "I'm sorry. Please excuse her. Mah Justine
has a vivid imagination."

Just in case, we faced the TV. We watched in
amazement as the reporter went nuts relating in explicit
detail how the flashing Sexy Santa tore off a skimpy St.
Nick costume. She danced naked as a jaybird with only
a string of blinking Christmas lights glued to her nipples
and playing Deck the Halls.

The camera focused on the mob of parade viewers
shoving one another as they jostled for a better position
to watch the bizarre scene unfold. The crowd surged and
a stampede ensued. At least a dozen spectators lost their
footing and were trampled by the mob. The screech of
sirens in the background drowned out the screaming of
the fallen victims.

The cameraman zoomed in for a close-up when the
parade procession stopped at the famous corner of
Hollywood & Vine. My eyes almost popped out of their
sockets as I watched two big LAPD uniforms leap onto
the float and hustle a half-naked *Sharon Hancock,* with
her illuminated boobs still flashing, and the choir belting
out Deck the Halls, off Santa's sled and arrest her.

Well, as they say in the South, shut mah mouth.

Merry Christmas to all and to all a good night…

Chapter Ten

Joan and Sonia were out of town visiting family between Hanukkah and Christmas and missed some of the industry intrigue and merriment madness. The rest of us stayed in town, busy buying last-minute gifts and attending holiday parties. The last time we'd gathered for our daily soiree? Lemme think. Yikes. Right before the Hanukkah party. So, we hadn't been together for a while. I distributed the morning coffee to the Yentas and raised my cup to toast our reunion.

Joan pointed a teaspoon at me. "Has your friend the Medical Examiner determined Leni Waxman's cause of death?"

I shook my head. "Regrettably, no. Multiple department employees took time off for the holidays. The coroner's office has been working with limited staff and many cases are backlogged."

Sonia's annoyance rang sharp in her tone. "Come on, Holly! This is the *Los Angeles County Coroner's Office that we're talking about here*. Not some Podunk hole in the wall where the local undertaker also acts as the Medical Examiner. Surely, they didn't schedule the *whole damned office* to be on holiday *at the same time*."

I held out my hands in supplication. "While death doesn't take a vacation, even the coroner's office staff is entitled to enjoy the holiday. Snip's chief technician as well as her assistant are both on vacation. The lab staff is down to one emergency technician and testing as well as analysis of the results are backed up by several days. I talked to Snip over the weekend. She said most staff are back from vacation this week and she would be conducting the autopsy on Leni today."

Hope arched a brow. "So, you're saying Dr. Cutler *isn't any further along* in her diagnosis than the night of the party?"

I shook my head. "Not exactly. Nothing official until they do a tox screen and a stomach contents assessment, and then get her on the table. Snip has a working theory based on the symptoms Leni displayed the night of the party, but she's not prepared to share it yet. We're having dinner tomorrow night. Hopefully, she will have something definitive by then."

I surveyed the table. "Any of you catch the Hollywood Stars Parade on Christmas Eve?"

Three headshakes and Hope bunched her shoulders. "I loved it as a little girl. But I outgrew the excitement of seeing Santa Claus and the stars don't impress me anymore."

I tsked, "Such a shame. Trust me, you're gonna kick yourselves for missing it. I turned on the TV and tuned onto KZLA to watch the parade while getting ready for my date with Miguel for Christmas Eve dinner with his family. A female dressed in a skimpy Santa Claus costume jumped on Santa's float and stopped the parade in its tracks." I glanced around the table. "The camera did a closeup and the woman performed a striptease!" I worked hard trying not to laugh. "And it focused on none other than a half-naked, drunk-looking *Sharon Hancock,* with flashing Christmas lights glued to her boobs and the choir belting out Deck the Halls. Miguel arrived at the same time the cops on TV jumped on the float and arrested Sharon."

Joan laughed hard enough that her chair tipped back so far, she had to grab onto the edge of the table to avoid falling on her ass. She used a crumpled napkin to wipe the tears running down her cheeks. "OMG! I'll never be able to sing *your namesake* Christmas carol again without bursting into laughter."

Queenie laughed and tried to talk at the same time. The result? A rather unladylike snort of coffee jetted out of her nostrils.

Sonia slapped the table so forcefully that she spilled everyone's coffee onto the table.

"Come again?" Hope twisted her head and smacked the side of it as though trying to drain water out of her ear. "Obviously, I didn't hear you right."

Sonia was the first to recover the ability to string a set of words together into a cohesive sentence. "Ah. *That* explains why Sharon went berserk at the party when Leni went after her."

Hope clucked her tongue. "Ah, what? Ah so?"

Sonia tapped the side of her head. "Remember, it was only after Leni called Sharon *Miss Flash* that Sharon went batshit crazy and lunged for Leni. Now it's understandable why Sharon went so nuts."

Hope held out her hands. "It is? Sorry, it's still clear as mud to me."

I snapped my fingers. "Sonia's right. This was no spur-of-the-moment stunt. The trick itself was carefully pre-planned and the timing of the feat was orchestrated with the precision of a measuring stick. I guess that the Christmas Eve parade incident wasn't Sharon's first flashing. And I bet my boat Leni knew all about it and held it over Sharon's head."

Queenie's jaw dropped. "You're saying Sharon is a *serial flasher*?"

I nodded. "Yes, indeedy."

Sonia stroked her chin. "So, if that's true, then Sharon had it right at the party. Leni Waxman *was* the type to use such information to destroy Sharon's life."

Queenie tapped her index finger on the tip of her nose. "If security didn't intervene, Sharon was angry enough to kill Leni bare-handed."

Joan smirked. "I bet she's pissed something else beat her to the punch."

Hope smiled at me. "So, on a happier note, did you enjoy Christmas Eve?"

I slapped a sincere-looking smile on my kisser. "The Nochebuena celebration was lovely. Delicious food and drink, festive decorations, lively music, and the Martinez family made me feel right at home."

Never one to miss a nuance, Eagle-eyed Joan observed me over the rims of her eyeglasses. "Yet why do I sense the word *but* is going to be the next one out of your mouth?"

Queenie tsked, "Because there usually *is one*. Why would this time be any different for the Olympic champion of complications?"

I funneled my lips. "Gee, Queenster, I appreciate the vote of confidence."

She bowed at the waist. "I live to serve."

As if Joan would let me wiggle out of a response. Yeah, right. Not in a million years.

Joan arched a brow. "So?"

I made a sour face. "The evening started rough and went downhill. As I said before, when he arrived, I wasn't ready yet and *Mr. Always Prompt* was annoyed."

Queenie looked at me oddly. "You're never late. Do you always keep *him* waiting?"

I shook my head. "Nope. This is the first time."

Joan tsked. "As if he's Mr. Perfect…"

Sonia pursed her lips. "He's a cop. If he is involved in a police matter and can't leave in the middle, he's kept you waiting a few times—right?"

I nodded.

Joan rolled her eyes. "So, what's his problem?"

"I made the mistake of letting him watch the parade incident and then we were off to the races."

Four sets of eyebrows shot up to their foreheads.

I held out my hands. "We watched the cops arrest Sharon and he no doubt remembered her name as a troublemaker from the Hanukkah party guest list. And I got a pre-emptive lecture on not interfering in Detective Jones' investigation."

I shrugged. "No clue if that's the case or if Miguel was only annoyed I went to the Hanukkah party with Buddy instead of him and is chastising me for my snubbing him in a way difficult for me to object to."

Joan pursed her lips. "Why do you say he was annoyed?"

"Because I'm sure he received a copy of the guest list and recognized *Buddy's name* on it. Since then, he's given me an earful whenever he has the chance."

Hope asked, "An earful about…?"

I wrinkled my nose. "My asking Buddy to the party and not Miguel."

Queenie huffed, "You're free to choose whoever you want to spend your time with. Last time I looked, you aren't one of his detectives Miguel can order around."

I grinned. "I guess he didn't receive the memo." I shrugged. "I tried to downplay not asking Miguel to accompany me to the Hanukkah party by saying I saved him from having a lousy time. He would either have been bored out of his gourd or as uncomfortable as a fish out of the water. I rationalized that Buddy is in the apparel industry and knew some of the suppliers and retailers. Buddy is relatively new to the LA apparel scene and the party was an excellent means to mingle and help move his career forward."

Joan blew the air out of her cheeks. "Not that you owed Miguel an explanation, but you gave him a perfectly logical one."

I held my hands out. "You're preaching to the Choir." I rolled my eyes. "The funny thing is, I didn't get the impression he particularly *wanted to go*. He just didn't want me going *with Buddy*."

Sonia rubbed her chin. "Sounds as if your Captain can't handle competition."

Hope waved her hands for a time-out. "Wait a minute. As of now, no investigation exists for you to interfere in—or am I missing something?"

"Yes, you're right." I bunched my shoulders. "The only thing I can figure is there's more to the situation than the cops are willing to say and he's doing an end around in case Leni's death becomes a police matter."

Hope widened her eyes. "The police suspect *Sharon* is responsible for Leni's death?"

Queenie scrunched her eyes. "Even if Leni's death turns out to be murder, the police *can't possibly* think Sharon is the killer. Security hustled her out of the ballroom way before Leni collapsed."

Joan teased. "So, which one of the men in your life will you be ringing in the New Year with?"

Hmm. The better question is which one do I *want*? Let's see. The last thing I want is the grief of bringing in the new year while drowning in drama. No competition from a dead spouse. No guff from nosy ghosts. No crap from controlling cops. Which one of the men in my life gets me to where I want to go? Only one.

Four blank sets of eyes stared at me as if I'd lost my mind. "The only one who *never* gives me any grief—Sigmund Freud Schlivnik!"

Chapter Eleven

The tantalizing aroma of garlic wafting in the air as the waiter delivered two steaming plates of ziti slathered in red marinara sauce to the table next to ours at the outdoor patio dining area of Pasta by the Pier made my mouth water. In case I missed the hint, my stomach growled loudly, reminding me that the tuna sandwich lunch I gulped down on the run from the mart to the factory earlier today was a distant memory.

Snip waved her menu like a flag. "Which dish looks good to you?"

I pointed to the left side of the menu. "I'm starving. This half of the menu will do it. And you?"

Snip narrowed her eyes. "I dunno. Normally I'd get my usual half pie and half pasta special, except I ate pizza last night."

"Why didn't you say something while we were discussing where to meet? We didn't have to go for Italian food. Burgers, Mexican, or Asian food are always okay by me."

Snip waved the idea away. "Nah, I love this place and besides, they offer a huge variety of choices." She opened the menu. "We've got a winner, ladies and gentlemen—eggplant parmesan. It's been ages since I've eaten it and this will be a nice change of pace."

"So, did you do takeaway or eat out?"

Snip said, "Ate out. I met Sherry Silverman at

Marino's Pizzeria in West Hollywood. You remember her, don't you?"

"If memory serves me correctly, she's a med school friend of yours we met for dinner at Antonio's last summer—right?"

Snip nodded. "Yep. Nothing's wrong with your memory. Sherry and I went through medical school together." Snip giggled like a naughty schoolgirl. "Sherry is a practical joker who can throw her voice. The first time our class went to the medical school morgue to do an autopsy, she thought it great fun to spook the other students. She waited until the meekest, most nervous guy in the class stood in front of the cadaver holding the scalpel in his shaking hand. Just as the guy finally worked up the courage to make an incision, Sherry threw her voice and yelped, '*Ouch! That. Hurts. Stop it*!' " Snip smacked the table and snorted a laugh. "The poor fella started shaking and turned white as a ghost. He dropped the scalpel into the cadaver's open midsection cavity and ran screaming out of the morgue. Half of the class followed him. Sherry was in hysterics. The dean didn't find her stunt the least bit funny and she had to do some serious begging not to be thrown out of medical school."

Sherry is my kind of gal. I applauded the stunt. "Diabolical yet brilliantly funny." I widened my eyes. "Thank the Goddess above Sherry didn't join you as a Medical Examiner." I slapped my cheeks. "Good gravy! She didn't, did she?"

Snip wiggled her brows. "Nope. She became a psychiatrist."

I burst out laughing. "How apropos and convenient! She can analyze her wacky behavior."

Snip shook her head. "Nah. No shrink ever analyzes

themselves or family or friends. They could never be objective. We swapped war stories and she shared one about her most interesting, if not, unusual patients."

I dipped my head. "Is it possible to do that and not violate the privacy laws?"

Snip nodded. "She never revealed the *identity of the patient*, so no privacy laws were broken. She only shared the patient's issue. The unusual part is that the patient is a *female* flasher. It is quite rare for a woman to have this particular personality trait. Statistically, flashers are *almost always men*."

I struggled to keep a blank expression.

Snip sighed. "The woman has been a patient of Sherry's for several years and despite some setbacks, she made some progress—until Christmas Eve. The holiday season is often a brutal time for people suffering from emotional problems. Something or someone triggered a terrible reaction in this woman and she went around the bend."

I slapped my cheeks. "Good grief. Please tell me she didn't commit suicide?"

Snip covered her right hand over her heart. "No, thank the Goddess, she didn't. But she did something so bizarre Sherry says it set her back psychologically years. Add the legal ramifications to her actions, and the woman may never fully recover."

My eyes bugged. "Legal ramifications? Did she flash a teller while robbing a bank?"

Snip held her index finger above her thumb. "Not quite, but you're this close. Sherry is on staff at Hollywood Medical Center Hospital and was on call Christmas Eve. Around nine o'clock she received notification one of her patients had been brought into the emergency room.

Sherry gets into the emergency room and sees her patient screaming at the top of her lungs for someone to help her. Accompanied by two LAPD uniformed cops—she's handcuffed behind the back, drunk as a skunk, wearing a skimpy Santa Claus costume torn to shreds—and half-naked with blinking Christmas lights glued to her nipples and Deck the Halls blaring from her boobs."

Snip dabbed her napkin across her face to wipe the tears of laughter trickling down.

"One of the ER nurses recognizes the flasher. She gets in front of her and calls her by her name. The nurse tries to calm the flasher down. Instead of calming down, the flasher goes berserk and shoves the nurse out of the way and she bumps into Sherry. Sherry falls on her ass and bounces across the room. As Sherry stands up, the woman kicks one of the cops in the nuts and then elbows the other one in the face and bloodies his nose. Since the woman flunked the sobriety test, Sherry couldn't sedate her with the usual tranquilizers. The cops held her down while Sherry sedated her using a tranquilizer made to calm spooked horses. Once they got the woman under control, Sherry had no choice and reluctantly signed the papers to transfer her patient to the jail ward at County General with the instruction, if necessary, to cuff her to the bed. Her patient was charged with indecent exposure, causing two car accidents, and disruption of a public event."

The lightbulb finally switched on inside Snip's head. She narrowed her eyes. "Who are you? *My Holly* would have asked a zillion annoying questions by now and be on the floor hysterically laughing. So, Miss Nosy—why no third degree?"

I held out my hands in supplication. No reason to continue my rope-a-dope routine. "I wanted to hear the whole story before I said anything. The only part of the story I didn't know was the scene in the hospital. I watched the Hollywood Star Parade on Christmas Eve night while getting ready for my date with Miguel. I observed the TV reporter go wild describing the woman dressed the way you said as she jumped onto the Santa Claus float Santa. She ripped open the top and flashed the world with her blinking boobs. Miguel arrived at the houseboat as the cops arrested the woman."

I sighed. "The camera did a close-up and I recognized her. The flasher is Sharon Hancock, a swimwear sales colleague recently fired by Leni Waxman."

Snip's jaw dropped.

I said, "Sharon attended the Hanukkah party and got into it hot and heavy with Leni Waxman. Security dragged Sharon out of the mart ballroom when she tried to take a swing at Leni."

Snip smiled tightly. "I guess LAPD and Sherry are going to buck heads over Ms. Hancock."

I asked, "Did you complete the autopsy on Leni Waxman today?"

Snip gave a sharp nod as she shoved half of the last breadstick in the basket into her mouth.

I gave her the big eyes. "So, are you gonna share the results or not?"

She held up a wait-a-minute gesture with her index finger and washed down the breadstick with a glug of wine.

"Doctor Levinson and numerous witnesses all described many of the early to mid-range classic symptoms of poisoning that Ms. Waxman exhibited the night of the party: Nausea and vomiting. Increased salivation. Abdominal pain. Pale skin color. Sweating. A rapid, heavy breathing called hyperpnea. Loss of full control of body movements called ataxia. Loss of balance and difficulty walking. Headache and dizziness. Muscle twitching. The early symptoms might come as early as fifteen minutes to an hour of contact with the poison. Death can occur within an hour of severe exposure. Death occurs due to paralysis of the muscles that control breathing. Fluid builds up in airways, heart, and blood vessel failures leading to cardiovascular collapse."

Snip shoved the other half of the breadstick into her piehole and crunched it to bits. While anxious for her to continue, history said my hurrying her along was pointless.

After swallowing another glug of wine, she continued. "The victim exhibited several later-stage symptoms such as muscle weakness, difficulty breathing, respiratory failure, and paralysis indicative of poisoning. Botulism, curare, tetrodotoxin toxicity, puffer fish, deadly nightshade, atropine, and scopolamine, Gelsemium, and nicotine could be the culprits."

I asked, "So were you able to identify which poison is responsible?"

Snip nodded. "Yes. We got lucky. We tested hair and skin samples and discovered enormous amounts of nicotine poisoning in her system absorbed through her skin."

I tapped my lower lip. "Smoking is prohibited in the ballroom—actually, smoking isn't allowed *anywhere* in the mart. If she's a heavy smoker, she must have smoked a ton of cigarettes before the party. A relatively short time—less than two hours passed— between her grand entrance into the ballroom and her collapse. For a woman her age, Leni kept herself in great shape. I'd never guess her to be a tobacco fiend. *How many* cigarettes would she need to smoke to die from nicotine poisoning in such a short time?"

Snip shook her head. "Ms. Waxman was not a smoker. Her lungs were healthy and clear."

I furrowed my brow. "So, how could the nicotine get into her system?"

"Her fingers and hands were coated with nicotine, as well as her lips, hair, and scalp. Maybe she vaped? Liquid nicotine is used in e-cigarettes. It is more concentrated in this form. E-cigarettes pose a bigger risk than smoking a cigarette. They use batteries to heat liquid nicotine — usually in a cartridge or container — into a gas or vapor so you inhale it. Swallowing this liquid nicotine can be toxic. It is also harmful if you spill some on your skin or get a little in your eye."

"So, you're saying she got the nicotine poisoning through her skin?"

Snip nodded.

I tapped my lower lip. "If that's the case and she vaped, maybe she did it before coming to the party. Since liquid nicotine is more concentrated, she'd use less of it than smoking a cigarette. Still, she probably vaped an awful lot to die from nicotine poisoning—right?"

Snip nodded. "Yes, but in this case percutaneous toxicity is the way the nicotine poisoning entered her body."

"What's per-cut-an-eous toxicity?"

"By the expression *percutaneous toxicity,* we refer

to the systemic poisoning following penetration of toxic materials through the cutaneous barriers and their distribution throughout the body."

I rolled my eyes. "*Plain English please*, Doctor Death."

Snip waved me off. "Sorry. In layman's terms, it means the poison gets into the body via the skin. The skin is an important portal of entry for many chemical substances. The two most important factors affecting absorption are the concentration of the applied chemical and the surface area of contact. Percutaneous toxicity is enhanced by delivering the largest concentration of agent over the greatest area. Percutaneous uptake will also usually increase if the skin has been damaged by the chemical."

I bit my lip. "Thinking back to the night of the party, Leni kept running her fingers through her hair and raking her scalp. I didn't count the number of times she did it. I bet she did it at least half a dozen times throughout the evening—maybe more. So, if she came into contact with a huge amount of nicotine, could it be absorbed into her system that way?"

Snip widened her eyes. "*Absolutely*. The scalp is *four times* more porous than the hand. Also, the frequency of the application, age, race, and general hydration of the skin have an impact because those areas of greater hydration have greater absorption. Contact poisons are those chemicals and toxins, such as nicotine, which are absorbed in sufficient quantities by direct skin contact to produce toxic effects, including death, in an individual. Nicotine is a toxic substance that affects various systems throughout the body. It raises your blood pressure and spikes your adrenaline, which increases your heart rate and the likelihood of having a heart attack. Nicotine poses several health hazards. There is an increased risk of cardiovascular, respiratory, and gastrointestinal disorders. Nicotine is quite a lethal compound. It's widely recognized to be deadly at doses between 30 and 60 milligrams, making it more dangerous than both arsenic and cyanide. Per the CDC: 50-60 milligrams is a deadly dose for an adult who weighs 150 pounds."

I said, "Leni was thin as a rail. Not an ounce of fat on her. She probably didn't weigh one hundred pounds soaking wet. So, it would take a lot less of the nicotine poisoning to kill her."

Snip nodded.

I asked, "So, where did she come into contact with the nicotine, and how did it get absorbed into her skin?"

Snip shook her head. "We don't know yet."

I asked, "You don't know if she came in contact with the nicotine inside or outside of the ballroom or you don't know where she came in contact with it at all?"

"Given the shortness of the time between when she entered the ballroom until she fell ill, we are confident she either came in contact with the nicotine poison right before she arrived at the ballroom or after she went inside. The CSI team collected every pot, pan, serving piece, utensil, dish, glass, and piece of silverware used at the party. They also bagged everything Ms. Waxman touched—her chair, the tablecloth at the head table, her dishes, glass, and silverware, the dais, her award, the dreidel, the library table, and all the door prizes she crashed into as well as her clothes and shoes. Everything is at the lab now being tested for nicotine."

I nodded. "Okay. Say you identify how she came

into contact with the nicotine poison. What next?"

"Then we can determine if it was an accidental overdose or something else."

I wrinkled my brow. "Or something else?"

Snip nodded. "If she got some help dying."

"Huh?"

Snip spelled each letter out with a flick of her fingers. "M-U-R-D-E-R."

Chapter Twelve

Eight P.M. Pacific Standard Time, New Year's Eve

I'm tucked in tight as a tick on my houseboat and snuggled into my comfiest elastic waistband sweats—perfect for guiltless holiday overeating indulgences. My tootsies are toasty warm in my trusty fleece-lined koala bear slippers.

I've ordered the extra-large noisemaker New Year's Eve special from Coast Pizza scheduled for delivery in an hour and chilled an expensive bottle of Champagne. Yum—nice and cold by the time the clock strikes midnight. To ensure a festive mood, I decorated the main salon with balloons and streamers and bought party hats and noisemakers. I'm a regular party animal...It's fifty-fifty if Siggie will wear his party hat. He may not be as party-hardy as me. We shall see.

I've gone from no men in my life to two smokin' hot ones chasing my ass all over town and both clamoring to bring in the new year with me. Any other woman on the planet with a pulse would kill to be in my shoes.

It's not as if I didn't receive any other offers. On the contrary—besides saying no to the two hot-to-trot-hunks, I also turned down a half-dozen dinner and party invitations. And here I am, poised to celebrate the arrival of the new year with Siggie as my date, and thrilled at the prospect. The Yentas and my mother all think I've lost my mind. Did I?

I chose not to go down that road, so I turned on the TV for a distraction. KZLA ran a live feed report from Pasadena on the frenzy of last-minute Rose Parade float preparations continuing throughout the night. Of course, seeing the broadcast brought me back to the Hollywood Star Parade debacle.

My dinner with Snip raised more questions than provided answers. On a hunch, I called my cousin Janie Goldberg, an emergency room nurse at Hollywood Medical Center Hospital. Her shift hours changed daily during the holidays, making it difficult to reach her. We'd been playing phone tag for three days.

My mother is an only child. Her mother was my beloved Nana, the eldest of six children. My Great-Aunt Bert is Janie's mother and the youngest of Nana's siblings. Bert is only sixteen years older than my mother. They were raised more as sisters than aunts and nieces in a two-family duplex in Brooklyn, New York. Janie and I are only two months apart and we were raised more like sisters than second cousins.

The KZLA telecast paused for a commercial break, and my gut tied in sailor's knots when the cell phone rang. Buddy? Miguel? Queenie? *My Mother*? Oye vey. Somebody, please shoot me. I snuck a reluctant glance at the caller ID and sighed with relief. Jane Goldberg, R.N.

"Hey, Janer! Honest to Goddess, this only took three freakin' days! The President of the United States is easier to get on the phone."

Janie laughed. "Let the president deal with loonies like the ones that come through my emergency room and then we've got something to talk about. Your message said you have some questions." Janie's tinkly laugh made the same sound as a spring creek as it meandered over rocks. "Is there some medical emergency at the mart?"

"Kind of...not exactly. Were you by chance on duty Christmas Eve?"

Jane said, "Due to an outbreak of the flu on staff here for almost a month now, we've been shorthanded at the worst possible time of the year. I've been on three-twelve-hour shifts between Christmas Eve and tonight, so the days are kind of fuzzy. I'm on lunch break right now. That's the night the flasher was brought into the emergency room, right?"

"Yes."

"Yep. I was on duty. Good golly Miss Holly, talk about a crazy night! A regular three-ring circus. Between a six-car wreck on the Hollywood Freeway and a gang fight on Highland Avenue, we already had a full house when the flasher arrived at the ER. The car wreck victims miraculously suffered only minor injuries and were in and out of the hospital in a couple of hours. We treated two gangbangers for gunshot wounds and transferred them to the jail ward at County General to spend Christmas as guests of the graybar hotel."

I said, "I watched the whole flasher-parade fiasco play out in real time on KZLA. The camera did a close-up and I recognized the flasher. She's a swimwear colleague of mine."

Janie said, "By the way...you're not the only one who recognized her. Despite her disheveled appearance, I recognized her immediately. We were once close friends."

It is a small world. "How do you know her?"

"Before she got into the apparel industry, Sharon studied to be a nurse."

My jaw dropped. That was the last thing on Earth I ever expected.

Janie asked, "So, your question is…?"

One question? Try a bazillion. "How bad was she?"

"The worst imaginable. Drunk and irrational. She still recognized me and was embarrassed for me to see her as such a mess. I tried to help her. Unfortunately, she lashed out and became physical with me and the rest of the ER staff. The doctor had to tranquilize her. It hurt my heart to see the disaster her life ended up in."

I asked, "You and Sharon went to school together?"

"Yes. We were both in the UCLA nursing program. We were lab partners from our freshman to junior years and spent a lot of time together."

"Why weren't you still lab partners in your senior year?"

"Because Sharon got married and dropped out of nursing school in the middle of our senior year."

"Geez, so close to graduation? If tuition money was the issue, I bet student loan options were available."

"Nope. Money wasn't the issue. She had the funds for tuition. She quit school to go to work full-time so she could put her husband through law school. We were close enough that they appointed me their children's Godmother. As time went on, we kept in touch as much as two busy friends who now traveled in different circles do. An occasional lunch. Mostly catching up type of phone calls. She never said it out loud, but she hinted that her husband resented any time she spent with her friends. Things seemed to be going okay for her for a while, then a year or two later I read between the well-practiced-sounding lines of news, weather, and sports and sensed not all was wonderful in paradise."

"Were you right?"

"Regrettably, yes."

"How so?"

"We met for lunch and honestly, I almost didn't recognize her. Dark circles under her eyes and the stooped, defeated posture of an old woman. She had aged ten years. She could tell that I noticed the changes in her. I asked if she had been ill and she burst into tears."

"Good gravy! How awful. Did she tell you why?"

Before Janie answered, a sharp rat-a-tat-tat knocked on the forward door. I checked the time. Janie and I were talking for almost an hour. No pre-delivery call from Coast Pizza to meet the delivery guy at the gate. Maybe he got lucky and someone let him in. Or my neighbor, Muriel changed her mind and accepted my invitation. I'd invited her to join me for pizza and champagne, but the feisty octogenarian declined, saying she would never make it to stay up so late.

I said, "Janie, lemme call you back. Somebody is at the door. It's probably the delivery guy with my pizza."

I hung up the phone and yelled, "Just a minute."

I opened the door and almost peed myself to find both Miguel and Buddy standing together, scowling at one another, each holding a magnum of champagne and a bouquet of daisies in the crooks of their arms.

New Year's Eve went downhill from there...

Chapter Thirteen

January 2nd

I pointed to the last day of last year's date on the West Coast Apparel News lying open in the middle of the Yenta table and swiped my wrist across my brow. "Whew. Thank the Goddess above *that year* is in the history books. I say good riddance. Goodbye and good luck." The stunned group sat transfixed as I related my New Year's Eve sad tale of woe.

"I'm in my comfy sweats and fuzzy slippers talking to my cousin Janie on the phone and there's a knock on the door. I assume it's the pizza delivery guy, but when I open the door, Buddy and Miguel are standing side by side each holding a magnum of Champagne and a bouquet of daisies and glaring at one another."

Hope asked, "Good grief! What did you do?"

I shrugged. "I stepped aside and let them in."

Queenie gasped, "*You invited them in?*"

I arched a brow. "Yeah. What would you do?"

Joan snarked, "Taken the booze and bouquets out of their arms, thanked them for the holiday cheer, and closed the door."

I rolled my eyes. "The way the two of them shoved one another as they jostled to get in and leave the other guy outside, it's a wonder they didn't push me overboard into the channel." I huffed. "Worse, they popped half of the balloons and tore down some of the streamers as they stumbled their way into crashing my party."

Sonia rubbed her chin. "Isn't your boat in a security basin and you need a key to open the gate?"

I nodded. "You're right. You do."

Sonia asked, "Did you give either of them a key?"

I slapped my cheeks. "*Good grief, no!* That's a big step I'm not ready to take with either of them yet."

Hope held out her hands. "So, then how did they get in?"

I said, "Miguel is a cop. He waited until one of my neighbors opened the gate and flashed his badge."

Joan laughed, "And Buddy? Miguel's bodyguard or his prisoner?"

Queenie twisted her lips into a wry smile. "From the sound of their antics, a little bit of both."

Sonia asked, "Okay, so once they boarded the boat, what in the world did you do?"

Joan used her fingers to make a pouring sign. "Since she already let the two clowns onto the boat, Miss Manners probably cracked open the bubbly and served a few rounds."

I grimaced. "Nope. I was too busy preventing them from smashing the champagne bottles over one another's heads. Despite the close quarters of a houseboat, they managed to circle one another like a couple of boxers trying to land the first punch."

Sonia rubbed her chin. "Maybe they drank too much before they got to the Marina?"

Hope said, "Certainly not together!"

I shook my head. "At least that would be an explanation for their stupid behavior. No, they acted dumber than two boxes of rocks, but both were sober as a couple of judges. Thank goodness for Siggie. My hound barked his head off when they started yelling and pushing and shoving one another around. Siggie got between Buddy and Miguel and kept them apart long enough for me to separate the two jerks."

Hope asked, "What were they yelling about?"

I batted my eyes. "Arguing as to which one of them I preferred!"

And as if this chaos wasn't enough, my two favorite ghosts arrived, urging me to choose Buddy and dump Miguel in the channel. Of course, I left the apparitions out of my ridiculous story. The Yentas would never believe me. Besides, who needs to add the woo-woo to the mix when the real story is already crazy enough?

Hope asked, "So, how did you end up getting rid of them?"

I laughed. "As it turned out, I didn't have to do anything. The situation took care of itself. They raised such a loud ruckus one of my dock neighbors called security. Two muscle-bound guards boarded my boat and asked the two Romeos for ID. Miguel flashed his badge and told security everything was under control. The guards paid no attention to his absurd assessment of the situation. Once I identified myself as the owner of the vessel, they asked if many more guests were expected and how much longer the party would go on. I said no more guests and the party *was over*. The guards escorted the Romeos self-righteously huffing and puffing off the boat…sans their booze and blooms."

Joan slapped the table. "*So, you drank all the champagne?*"

Sonia said, "That's a lot of champagne for one woman." She grinned. "Good thing you were already home because you'd never pass a sobriety test."

I wiggled my eyebrows. "Nah. That was too much to drink alone. I ordered three more pizzas and invited all the neighbors in my basin over as an apology. Mark next door brought a boom box and voila, a spur-of-the-moment dock party. We scarfed down the pizzas, guzzled all the champagne, and danced up and down the gangplank into the wee hours of the night. Muriel came down in her robe and curlers to celebrate. Siggie acted as the four-legged master of ceremonies. He scampered from person to person spreading his canine brand of holiday spirit." I raised my coffee cup in a toast. "It turned out to be one of the best New Year's Eve celebrations ever."

My smile dimmed. "By the time the dock party broke up, Janie had gone off her shift and I didn't want to risk waking her if I called her at home. I wanted to hear the end of her Sharon story, so yesterday, I met Janie for breakfast at the Rainbow City Café across the street from the hospital before she started her shift." I surveyed the table. "Sharon's story is enough to break your heart. Sharon and my cousin were in nursing school together. In her senior year, Sharon got married and quit the nursing program. She gave up a career in something she loved to put her husband through law school. An uncle of hers in the fabric business fronted Sharon into a sales job at Rapido. She did extremely well and rose to the role of VP of sales. After he passed the bar, her husband got recruited by a major law firm and fast-tracked for a partnership. Once the two children came along as well as the entertaining responsibilities of a partner's wife, Sharon's chance to go back to nursing school had passed. The husband is now a high-powered attorney and made a full partner in record time. He has a reputation for being a killer in the courtroom and having a roaming eye.

"After a buyer rescheduled a meeting, Sharon arrived home early from work one day and found the husband in their bed with his secretary. Sharon filed for divorce, and the husband left her with nothing in a messy public trial. Leni knew all about it because Sharon took so much time off work. Heartless Leni fired Sharon right in the middle of the trial and gave her a pittance of a lawsuit-saving severance. Almost destitute, and desperate, Sharon told Janie she had nothing left to lose. So, she made her husband pay big time."

My grin stretched as wide as a Jack O'Lantern. "She strolled into the conference room in her husband's law firm as if she owned the place —dressed to the nines in an expensive business suit and carrying a stack of legal-looking documents —and interrupted a meeting with an important, conservative client. The client probably assumed she was her husband's secretary— until she jumped up onto the conference table and ripped her shirt open revealing her size double D tits. Then she jumped down and cupped her big boobies in her palms and shoved her bare chest inches away from the client's face and twirled the girls for a full-frontal effect. Security came and dragged Sharon out of the conference room, but the damage was already done.

"The outraged client fired Sharon's ex-husband on the spot and took his business to another firm. As a result, Sharon's ex almost lost his job, let alone a partnership. Only because his firm chose to avoid the notoriety brought by bad publicity, the police weren't called and no criminal charges were made against Sharon. Her ex-husband sued her for custody of the kids. He based his case on that as a flasher, she was an unfit mother. The court agreed and now Sharon is only permitted supervised visits twice a month with her kids. Sharon accused her ex of giving the information to Leni who used it against her in the market and made it almost impossible for Sharon to get another job. The flashing became more frequent. Sharon started seeing a therapist and making progress. Regrettably, the emotion of the holiday season and her fight with Leni pushed Sharon over the edge."

Queenie tapped her fingernail in a rat-a-tat-tat beat on her coffee cup. "Leni and Sharon's ex-husband are both lucky all Sharon did was flashing. Desperate people often make terrible decisions. Sharon made many, and she paid dearly for them. Imagine if she started sharpshooting instead of flashing…"

Chapter Fourteen

Patience has never been one of my strong suits, but if I wanted the update on Leni Waxman's cause of death, experience dictated I put a smile on my face and zip my lips while Doctor Death chomped down at least half of her Coast Burger Special before she'd pony up any news.

Moments before I would split my spleen from anticipation, my favorite forensic finally raised her head from her clean-as-a-whistle plate. She swiped the crumpled corner of a grease-stained paper napkin across her chops to chase an errant smudge of catsup dribbling down her chin.

I gave her the move it along already twist of a wrist. "Okay, Wimpie. Before I expire from curiosity, give me the four-one-one on Leni Waxman's cause of death."

She gulped a glug of Chardonnay and donned her professor's cap. "The tox test results made my hypothesis conclusive. Ms. Waxman died as a result of a mixture of nicotine and dimethyl sulfoxide— commercially recognized as DMSO— the mixture produced a poison, which was absorbed across the skin after the victim contacted it."

"What's DMSO?"

"Dimethyl sulfoxide—better known as DMSO— has been used for medical treatment and as a pharmacological agent in humans since the 1960s. Today, DMSO is used mostly for cryopreservation of stem cells, treatment of interstitial cystitis, and as a penetrating vehicle for various drugs. The pharmaceutical industry developed drug delivery systems, which enhance the percutaneous absorption of various drugs. These agents include Dimethyl Sulfoxide (DMSO), Azone (Laurocapram), Propylene glycol, and N-methyl pyrrolidone. Solvents like DMSO facilitate the penetration of toxicants through the skin by increasing the permeability of the barrier layer of the skin, principally by disrupting the lipid layers. Nicotine is a toxic substance. It raises your blood pressure and spikes your adrenaline, which increases your heart rate and the likelihood of having a heart attack. The mixture of DMSO and nicotine is an extremely effective contact poison."

My eyes widened. "So, someone *purposely added* this DMSO stuff to speed up the absorption of the nicotine into Leni's body?"

Snip nodded.

My jaw dropped. "So, you're saying Leni was *murdered?*"

Snip made a ta-da with her hands. "Yes, ma'am. Ms. Waxman was a healthy woman. She had *no medical reason* to ingest DMSO in any strength. And the *only reason* to mix DMSO and nicotine is to shorten the amount of time it takes to poison someone."

"You informed Detective Jones?"

Snip nodded. "I faxed him my report and the test results earlier today."

I asked, "If you're not a pharmacist or in the medical field, is it difficult to get this stuff?"

Snip held out her hands. "Not difficult at all. A number of these solvents are commercially available.

DMSO is available at big box stores. Liquid nicotine is used by those who vape using E-cigarettes, so it is easily obtained from several suppliers."

"I'm not familiar with DMSO. If you're not in the medical field, despite being easy to buy, how does the average Joe know to use it to speed up the poisoning process?"

Doctor Death smiled grimly. "A quick online inquiry gives a murderer all the information they need."

I asked, "How did Leni come in contact with the poisonous mixture?"

"The lab tested hundreds of items. Virtually everything we tested—from the caterer's utensils to each guest's place setting— turned out clean. The victim's clothes, shoes, chair, and table setting all indicated various trace levels of the poison, except one item."

Snip grinned and raised her right hand as though a witness in court. "Trust me, we medical examiners can't make this stuff up. Believe it or not, the *dreidel* was completely coated with several layers of the poisonous mixture."

I patted my cheeks. "The night of the party, Leni was *all over the dreidel*. She rubbed her hands and fingers over each of its four sides to explain the significance of each Hebrew letter while teaching the guests how to play the game. She clutched it to her chest and kissed it for good luck before she gave it a spin. And she raked her fingers across her scalp at least a dozen times." I laughed. "This certainly puts a *whole new spin* on the Hanukkah dreidel game."

****

The next morning, I stopped at the newsstand outside the Mart Deli, bought the latest edition of the

West Coast Apparel News, and headed to A Jolt of Java. After a stop at the barista station to pick up our pre-paid beverages, I made my way through the crowded shop to the Yenta table.

I served the coffee, laid the newspaper across the center of the table, and pointed to the headline: *Waxman Whacked. No Suspects*

The Yentas listened attentively as I recapped the results of Snip's autopsy findings. It spoke to legions about the low opinion much of the industry held for Leni Waxman. No one, including the Yentas and the press, seemed particularly taken aback at Snip's diagnosis of murder.

Queenie shrugged. "This is no big surprise. If only *half* of the awful things they say she did are true, it's a miracle this didn't happen sooner."

Joan peered at the headline over the rims of her glasses and snarked. "*Whacked*? Good gravy! If you go by the headline, Leni Waxman was a Mafia Boss rubbed out by a rival gang instead of a swimwear manufacturer."

Sonia stroked her chin. "In many ways, she behaved like a Mafia boss."

Hope widened her eyes. "Granted, she was a nasty one but *a Mafia boss*? A bit over the top, no?"

Sonia pursed her lips. "Not in the least. Leni Waxman was as territorial as a gangster. She used the same methods— extortion, intimidation, and threats to protect her fiefdom at all costs and destroy her rivals the same way as a mobster. She found the weaknesses in people and used those defects to defeat her competitors and force her will on customers, employees, sales staff, and suppliers. A predator who stopped at nothing to retain her top-dog position, she never gave a rat's ass if she eviscerated a sales rep's career or destroyed a competitor in the process."

Joan held out her arm. "So, the list of potential murderers is as long as my arm."

Queenie said, "The TV detectives always say to follow the money."

Sonia ticked the most obvious candidates off with a tap of a teaspoon. "On TV the family members are always the prime suspects."

Hope arched a brow. "I dunno. At the party, they looked like a nice family who loved each other."

I twirled my teaspoon on the table edge. "According to Gary, it was an act and the Waxman family would never be confused with the Cleavers or the Waltons."

Joan bunched her shoulders. "Okay, so they're not the all-American family. Big deal. It's a stretch from not singing kumbaya together twenty-four-seven to one of her family bumping off Leni."

Sonia tapped her lower lip. "California is a community property state. If Leni's husband divorced her, they'd still split everything they *acquired together* down the middle. If the money to fund the business came from moolah Leni brought into the marriage, then she'd get to keep the business." Sonia rubbed her chin. "So, if the husband wanted it all, divorce was not the answer. The only way he'd get everything is if his wife died. Sounds like a dandy motive to me…"

Queenie shook her head. "I dunno. Morty didn't strike me as the one who wore the pants in that marriage. I don't see a Casper Milquetoast kind of guy like him having the gumption to knock off a powerhouse wife like Leni Waxman."

Hope pursed her lips. "And Leni's children?"

Joan pushed her glasses up to the bridge of her nose. "Nah. The kids make no sense. Leni's no spring chicken. The kids are going to inherit everything sooner or later. Why kill Leni since she's close to retirement age? Besides, older people *do* just get sick and die."

Queenie tapped her index finger on the tip of her nose. "Who had the most to lose?"

I ticked off the list on my fingers. "Between the suppliers—Elena Sosa who Leni threatened to take her business elsewhere, to the fired employees—Sharon Hancock, to competitors she tried to run out of business—Allen Brown"

Queenie nodded. "We definitely have to consider Allen Brown. And you might be right about Elena. She is a Cuban-American originally from Miami. Elena mentioned to Gary that as a teenager she spent summers in Tampa at her family's tobacco farm. Her uncle is a cigar manufacturer who taught Elena how to make cigars. So, she has *lots of experience* with nicotine."

I nodded and continued my list. "And the retailers like Carefree Casuals, and Goliath Sporting Goods. And you better put the Allied Department Store Chain at the *top of the list* after Leni killed the competition swim portion of their season thanks to her product's crappy store-within-a-store performance. So, maybe the better question to ask is *who didn't have* the most to lose?"

Hope's jaw dropped so low it almost hit the table. "*Allied Stores*? As in Bainbridge Department Stores? As in Sue Ellen Magee? *That Allied Stores*?"

Is there more than one?

I nodded. "Yes, indeedy. Leni had no problem taking from Paul to give to Peter to increase her customer base beyond Sporting Goods stores and Universities. She approached Allied Stores and pitched a competitive swim business. She convinced them to bring in four vendors as the base supplier matrix. She created an attractive program of inside prices not offered to her other retail customers. In exchange, Rapido received the largest orders and was the only vendor given a store within a store. Since the corporation made the decision, whether they wanted to be in the competitive swim business or not, individual chains, including *Bainbridge,* were obligated to comply."

Sonia snapped her fingers. "You know what? *I remember this.* I was in Sue Ellen's office the day the directive came down from corporate. While the competitive swim category got separate funding and didn't come out of her fashion budget, Sue Ellen ranted and raved about not having the competition swimwear customer, let alone any additional room on her floor for an untested category. To her utter consternation, her concerns fell on deaf ears. And to add insult to injury, Leni convinced Allied corporate to allow *her to write* the Rapido orders."

I said, "A corporate decision is beyond her control—yet I can't wrap my brain around *Sue Ellen Magee ever* agreeing to let a vendor pick the styles and write her orders."

Always one to look for the silver lining, Hope said, "On the bright side, after the Rapido goods died on the floor, at least Sue Ellen couldn't be held responsible for the calamity."

Joan nodded. "True, however, the competitive swimwear ultimately hurt Sue Ellen's profit margins across the board. Rapido's poor sales dragged down the margins for the other three better-performing competitive swim lines and the overall department margin was negatively impacted as well. And if she wanted to reorder a hot style, she had no place on her sales floor to put it due to all the unsold Rapido taking up valuable space."

Sonia raised her brows. "So, by my calculations, around fifty potential killers for the police to sort through."

Queenie smiled grimly. "Better make it fifty-one."

Hope cocked her head. "Who?"

Queenie choked on the name. "G-Gary makes the top of the list."

Chapter Fifteen

Three Days Later

Queenie shrugged out of her jacket and sat in a chair across from me at a tiny table for two best described as "ladies' room adjacent" in the far corner of the packed Mart Deli. She hung her purse strap on her chair back and scowled as her perfectly manicured index fingernail tapped the tabletop. "Geesh, is there a table *any smaller than this one*? Better plan to take turns eating because this one can't hold more than one plate at a time."

I shrugged. "The place is only open for breakfast and lunch. Their limited hours and the volume-based nature of their business are dependent on turning the tables. They don't want you getting too comfortable and taking up a spot all day."

She smacked the table edge with the heel of her hand. "They certainly ensured *that from never* happening." She wrinkled her nose as two women pushed against her on their way to the ladies' room. "Lunchtime should be a relaxing experience to revitalize you for the rest of the day."

I laughed out loud. "If that's your idea of lunchtime, you are in the wrong business."

Queenie pursed her lips. "Unless we get here ahead of the lunch crowd, I'm not interested in coming back and cramming myself into a corner halfway inside the ladies' room." She jutted her chin. "This isn't the only game in town. There *are* other places to eat."

I twisted my lips into a sly grin. "I agree…however, for a couple of Nosy Nellies like us, this is the *best place* to scope out the latest news. While waiting for our table, I ran into a rather chatty Allen Brown who *couldn't wait* to spill the beans on the latest Rapido gossip. Hadassah Waxman is now running Rapido. She officially took over two days ago and has already made some huge changes."

Queenie wrinkled her brow. "What kind of changes?"

"Cleaning house. The first day she took over the company's reins, she fired anyone and everyone loyal to Leni."

Queenie tapped her index finger on the tip of her nose. "I dunno. Being new at the helm, it seems as though she'd want the most experienced team around her."

I funneled my lips. "Looks like Rapido just traded in one my-way-or-the-highway CEO for another less-experienced one."

Queenie asked, "So, who killed Leni?"

I held my nose as if I'd taken a whiff of yesterday's garbage. "This one has the stink of a revenge murder. My money is on Sharon Hancock. Leni didn't merely fire an employee for cause. She destroyed Sharon's career."

Queenie nodded. "I agree Sharon is a prime candidate, however, if revenge is the motive, other equally qualified suspects can't be discounted. Elena Sosa and Allen Brown are two candidates who must make the list. Leni did as much to ruin them as she did Sharon. The question is why?"

I smiled sardonically. "Answer that question and Leni's killer is toast."

****

After lunch, Queenie and I went to the factory to prepare for our weekly production meeting. We just started to make a list of work-in-process update questions when our assistant Harriet opened the top of the split breezeway door separating her office from ours. "Ladies, the receptionist called and said LAPD Detective Jones is in the lobby." Harriet stuck her head through the breezeway opening. "He's here to see *Gary*."

Queenie narrowed her eyes. "Does he have a warrant?"

Harriet said, "The receptionist didn't say so. Do you want me to ask?"

Does he need one? Do we demand he produce one? Nah, it only makes Gary look guilty.

I waved the thought off with a flip of a wrist. "No. Tell the receptionist to give him a visitor's badge and have him wait for an escort to the design studio. Go up to reception in five minutes and take him to the design room the long way around the building perimeter. This will give us some time to prep Gary so he doesn't freak out."

Harriet gave us the thumbs up and reached for the phone receiver.

Queenie drummed her fingers on her desk. "Do we need to call Ms. Markowitz?"

After Queenie was wrongly arrested for Mermaid's former CEO Butch Oldham's murder, she needed a lawyer. My Uncle Barry, a personal injury attorney in Beverly Hills, sang Rose Markowitz's praises. *"If I ever found myself in trouble with the law, Rose Markowitz is the one attorney I'd ever call."* Trusting my uncle's judgment completely, I put Queenie's life in Ms.

Markowitz's capable hands. Thank the Goddess. The diminutive octogenarian criminal defense attorney extraordinaire kicked the homicide detective's ass and saved Queenie's tush. If Gary's tush needs saving, my money is on Ms. M.

I shook my head. "Not yet. Right now, all Jones wants to do is interview Gary. It would look as if Gary has something to hide if we involve a lawyer now. If it gets ugly then we bring Ms. M. in." I stood and angled my head to the door. "Let's get down to the design studio."

****

We calmed Gary down and prepared him as much as possible. Queenie advised him on the way to respond while being interviewed by the police—stay calm, only answer the questions asked, don't embellish, don't volunteer anything, don't get defensive, and don't go after the detective.

I sent Queenie back to our office to finish working on our production meeting prep and instructed her to keep Ms. Markowitz's number ready to dial if I gave her the high sign. I circled the factory via the perimeter walkway connecting all parts of the building and returned to the design studio from the opposite end. I plastered my body perpendicular to the outside wall at the entrance to the studio to see in and not be seen. Detective Jones sat across from Gary at a design work table.

Jones smiled at Gary as he took a small notepad and nub of a pencil from his inside jacket pocket, but the smile never made it to the detective's eyes. "I appreciate your taking the time to see me, Mr. Burkett." Jones waved at the piles of fabric swatches laid across the work table. "I see you are busy, so I'll try not to take too much of your time."

Gary nodded and Jones flipped the notebook to a clean page and poised the pencil, ready to write. "You knew Ms. Waxman?"

Gary nodded.

"How did you know her?"

"I worked for her."

"Recently?"

"No, just out of design school."

"How long ago did you graduate?"

"It will be ten years this coming June."

"In what capacity did you work for Ms. Waxman?"

Gary raised his brows and smiled as he fingered the fabric swatches on the table. "Well, Detective Jones, I said I worked for Ms. Waxman after I graduated from *design school…*"

I internally cheered. "Good on you, Gary! Don't let the wiseass cop get away playing stupid games." The annoyed expression on Jones' face said Gary would pay a price for his indulgence.

Jones tapped the closest pile of swatches to him with his pencil eraser. "I understand, Mr. Burkett. However, as a newbie, for all I know, Ms. Waxman might have started you out cutting fabric swatches. So do us both a favor and quit jerking me around and *answer the question.*"

Gary smiled. "I thought I did. For your clarification, I worked for her first as an assistant designer. I was promoted to head designer after Hattie O'Neal retired."

"How long did you work for Ms. Waxman?"

"Six total years. Two as the assistant designer and four as the head designer."

Jones scratched a note in the book and looked up. "A dream job. Why did you leave?"

"I didn't leave. I was let go."

"Why?"

Gary dipped his head. "Differences in approach to design plan."

"Meaning?"

"The design trends of the competition swimwear market changed from traditional to more fashionable, but Leni wouldn't allow me to make any revisions to Rapido's master design plan. Leni's philosophy? Rapido was the industry leader other vendors followed, not the reverse."

"Please clarify."

"Leni's approach was if it ain't broke, don't fix it. Mine is to look forward, not backward. Two theories of design won't work if they are the antithesis of one another."

Jones leaned forward in his seat. "After all the effort you put into designing Ms. Waxman's products, I bet you were furious at her for firing you." Jones glared at Gary. "Were you, Mr. Burkett? *Were you furious at her?*"

Gary shrugged, "Not in the least. Disappointed perhaps. Furious? No way. She owned the company, not me. She made a designer change to a person who was a better fit for her product vision. It happens all the time in this industry."

"Severance?"

Gary nodded. "Industry standard. Two months."

"So, you'd say you two parted amiably?"

"Yes."

Jones closed the notebook and stood up. "Thank

you, Mr. Burkett. That's all the questions for today. We're at the beginning of the investigation. Please make yourself available if additional questions arise."

Gary swept an arm around the studio. "You know where to find me, Detective."

Chapter Sixteen

I turned to rearrange the samples back into the correct order on the workstation rack after Sue Ellen Magee's appointment. My back stiffened at the sound of the soft lilt of a familiar Southern accent that, damned it, still thrilled me beyond all reason. "Hello, Holly Swimsuit. I've missed you."

I didn't see hide or hair of Buddy after the infamous New Year's Eve altercation. It took guts to come by after his performance. I'd give him credit for courage. So, I turned around to face him.

I arched a brow. "Are you in the mart working and just stopped by, or is something on your mind?"

The normally cool-as-a-cucumber Cajun shuffled his feet like a nervous teenage boy mustering up the courage to ask a girl to the prom. "U-uh. S-something o-n m-my m-mind."

I gave him an expectant look and made a go-ahead sign by twirling my wrist in a circle. Buddy remained mum and found something fascinating to stare at on the floor.

The electricity of anticipation arced across the room and a blanket of tension hung low in the air the way humidity does at high noon on a sizzling August Miami day. I crossed my arms akimbo over my girls and tapped the toe of my shoe in a rat-a-tat beat against the peg and groove wooden floor. I cleared my throat and he looked up. His eyes followed my fingers as I touched the face of my watch. Twelve-fifteen.

"I realize it's short notice," He pointed to the showroom door. "I'm hoping you're free for lunch."

He caught me off-guard and I wasn't ready to deal with him yet. My first inclination? To say I already made lunch plans. Yet curiosity got the best of me. Besides, a free meal is a free meal...I'd been in the mood for a Dale's Secret Harbor seafood salad for ages, but who wants to sell a kidney to pay for a meal? Now that I am a business owner, everything is on me. One of Mr. Bigshot's designer's perks is an expense account.

I made a decision and squared my shoulders. You've got something to say? No problemo. Lunch it is...you can bet your bottom dollar it's gonna cost you, Buddy boy...and trust me, the salad is gonna be the *least expensive* part of the meal.

I flashed a million-dollar smile and tucked my arm into the crook of his elbow. "Ever eaten the seafood salad at Dales? If not, then today is your lucky day."

****

We sat across from one another in an intimate dark maroon leather booth in the back of the fancy restaurant. We ate companionably as he babbled on throughout the delicious meal about news, weather, and sports...anything other than the subject in question. Once the busboy cleared the table and the waiter poured a refill on the coffee, I'd used up every ounce of patience. I pointed to my watch again and smirked. "They call it lunch *hour* for a reason." I made another *get-on with it already* twists of a wrist. "So, spit it out already."

A flare of scarlet red embarrassment traced from his neck to his widow's peak as he flashed an aw-shucks grin of his that still curled my toes. Damn him. He traced a fingertip across my palm and the world momentarily went sideways. Good grief, Schlivnik...get a grip on yourself.

"I-Ive wanted to call and..." The words clogged in his throat as his eyes searched mine for...? A suggestion? My phone number? Forgiveness? A get-out-of-jail card? Good luck, Buddy Boy. If he sang the I'm So Sorry song in the right key, I might be inclined to forgive him...however, nowhere did it say I had to make it easy for him...

He flinched as I cocked a brow. "What stopped you?"

Before he replied, the waiter dropped the check in the middle of the table. Buddy reached for it and clucked his tongue as he reviewed it. "Crap," he waved the check in the direction of the waiter's disappearing backside. "The guy left the wrong check." Buddy stood up and semi-shouted to the waiter's receding backside, "Excuse me, sir, this isn't our check." He turned to me. "I'll be right back." He waved the check in the air. "Sit tight. This won't take more than a minute or two."

As Buddy marched toward the reception desk, the temperature at the booth dropped fifty degrees as my two favorite ghosts swirled down and sat on either side of me.

Marie LaValle pointed to Buddy and pursed her lips into a funnel. "What in the Sam Hill is your problem, woman? Cut the poor boy some slack, for Heaven's sake. Are you deaf or just plain dumber than a box of rocks?"

My cheeks went numb as she blew a big puff of cold air in my face to make her point.

"Cain't you see mah Cajun Boy is tryin' his level best to make amends?"

Little Justine protruded her adorable lower lip. "Daddy is so sad without you. Please forgive him. He didn't mean to act bad."

Marie jutted her chin. "You wasn't raised in a barn, so at least have the decency to hear the poor boy out."

Before I had the chance to tell Marie to mind her own beeswax, the two ghosts disappeared as Buddy took his seat across from me. He swiped the back of his hand across his forehead. "Okay. The bill is straightened out."

Those two cute dimples of his that always make my knees go weak cratered his cheeks as he flashed a lopsided smile. "Now where did I leave off? Oh yeah…"

****

I served the Yentas their coffee the following morning and held my cup up. "Drink up, ladies. Once you're sufficiently caffeinated, I've got an interesting story to share."

Joan peered over the tops of her eyeglasses and smirked. "I prefer sipping coffee, not slurping. How much Java are we talking about?"

Sonia stroked her pointy chin. "Joanie's right." She waved her fingers into air quotes. "Do we need a refill to prep for another *Schlivnik adventure*? Only one cup? Two cups? A pot for each of us?"

Queenie funneled her lips. "No kidding. And another Schlivnik adventure to only where the Goddess above knows?"

I pursed my lips. "Don't get your panties in a bunch."

The Yentas displayed an annoying, yet understandable reluctance to hear the details of my tale with a group groan. Four sets of eyes rolled as synchronized as a high school drill team.

I shrugged. "It's not another *Schlivnik adventure*. After Sue Ellen left the showroom yesterday, I was in the middle of putting the line back in order and *Buddy* arrived and invited me to lunch."

Hope widened her eyes. "No kidding! When was the last time you saw him?"

I dipped my head. "The New Year's Eve debacle. I wasn't ready to deal with him yet and almost said I already made lunch plans..." I grinned. "But curiosity got the best of me, and let's face it, a free lunch is a free lunch."

Joan smirked. "Lemme guess. You suggested Dales."

I laughed sardonically. "Where else?"

Sonia asked, "So, what was on Buddy's mind besides lunch?"

"Some industrial-strength groveling for forgiveness and..."

Hope clapped her palm over her heart and gasped, "OMG! I bet he proposed! Did he hide the engagement ring in the breadbasket for you to find? Did he drop on one knee and ask for your hand like in the movies? Did you say yes?"

Joan shoved two fingers in her mouth and made the international gag sign.

Queenie grabbed my left hand and pointed to my naked ring finger. "Well, if he did propose, the cheapskate didn't spring for an engagement ring."

I snatched my hand out of her grasp. "Good gravy! Before you all go jumping to conclusions, give a girl a chance to explain." I wiggled my digits under their noses. "No, he did *not* propose. As to his groveling for forgiveness, we're not home yet."

Joan clucked her tongue. "*That's it?*"

Honestly, Joan? First, you're worried about the wildness of the story and then you're disappointed by the lack of excitement of the tale. Some days there is no pleasing this group. Geesh.

I held up an index finger. "When he walked me back to the showroom, he asked if he could come to the boat after work to discuss something important. He wouldn't give me so much as a small hint of the subject matter, but said it would be worth my time…*and he'd bring dinner.*" I surveyed the table. "It sounded like an ingenious way to set up round two of '*please take me back*'. Yet once again, curiosity and another free meal compelled me to say okay. He showed up at seven sharp carrying two bulging bags of Blue China Moon takeout, a couple of bottles of wine, and a stuffed manila envelope. We polished off the food and wine in no time. After we cleaned up the galley, Buddy brought out the envelope. I brewed a pot of coffee and he shared something remarkable…"

I glanced around the table and giggled. "Do you guys remember at the Hanukkah party for someone who isn't Jewish, Buddy sure seemed to know an awful lot about the holiday?" Four heads nodded and I continued. "After the party, a call to his Mee-maw for information only led to more questions. So, he signed onto one of those genealogy sites and found his family history on his mother's side." I widened my eyes. "You're not going to believe it…Buddy's maternal ancestors, the Benveniste family, were *Jews* who lived in Zaragoza in the Basque region of *Spain*. Buddy discovered that Benveniste was a popular pre-expulsion Sephardic Jewish surname. During the Inquisition, the Benveniste family became

Conversos."

Hope asked, "What is a Converso?"

I said, "To avoid being persecuted, these Jews *pretended* to convert to Catholicism. In reality, they practiced Judaism secretly. Despite all their precautions, his family's true faith was discovered. To escape prosecution and possible execution, they fled to Toulouse, France by way of Andorra. Through several generations, his family integrated into French society, and little by little, the Jewish traditions they left Spain to continue to practice became diluted and they did not understand the reason why, but they continued to celebrate them. His maternal ancestors immigrated to the United States and arrived in Louisiana as French-speaking Catholics. Or so they thought..."

Joan peered at me over the tops of her eyeglasses. "Or so they thought?"

I smiled, "According to Jewish law, we take the surname of our fathers and the *religion* of our mothers. So, technically, Buddy is *Jewish*."

Queenie burst out laughing. "Well, he didn't propose yet, but I bet your mother already ordered the wedding invitations."

Oye vey.

Chapter Seventeen

I got stuck behind a railroad crossing on Olympic Blvd. a few blocks west of our factory. Twenty minutes later the last car of the train finally passed and I careened into the Mermaid Swimwear parking lot on two wheels and slid into my parking space.

I waved to the receptionist and speed-walked down the hall to the executive wing. As I reached the office suite Queenie and I shared, I checked the time—crap, almost a half hour late for our weekly management meeting. I pushed the door open and stopped short. The room was empty. Not a soul sat at the conference table.

I opened the passway separating our office from Harriet's and stuck my head in. In an attempt not to kill the messenger, I fought to keep the annoyance out of my tone. "Harriet, this is a *mandatory weekly meeting* scheduled for the *same time and same place*, so all attendees are aware of when and where to show up. So, where the Sam Hill is everyone? I'm only late because I got stuck at a railroad crossing waiting for a long freight train to pass. Why didn't Queenie start the meeting without me?"

Harriet pursed her lips. "She did."

I pointed to the empty conference table. "Twelve execs plus Queenie, you, and me each one to present a report sit in at this meeting. Unless they all speed-talked or had nothing to report, they should only be a quarter of the way through the meeting. So, why am I the only one in the room?"

Harriet sighed. "We'd no sooner started the meeting and the receptionist called to say Detective Jones was in the lobby."

"What did he want this time?"

Harriet sighed. "To see Gary again."

"Since he didn't call in advance to schedule the interview, why not excuse yourself, go to the lobby, and ask Jones to either wait until the meeting was over or come back after lunch?"

Harriet's back stiffened. "*I did.*"

"And?"

"And after I presented the two options, let's say he wasn't in a conciliatory mood…"

I made a sour face. "Meaning?"

Harriet's shoulders slumped. "Meaning, he got testy and said he could interview Gary here at the factory or he'd take him back to the precinct, but either way, Gary is skipping the meeting."

"And then?"

She shrugged. "And then I called Queenie."

"*And?*"

"And five minutes later Gary came to the lobby."

"Did Jones take Gary to the precinct?"

"No. The receptionist gave Jones a visitor pass and he followed Gary back to his office."

I arced an arm to the conference table. "So, where is everyone else?"

Harriet said, "I returned to the conference table as Queenie announced something unavoidable came up and rescheduled the meeting for two this afternoon."

"Where's Queenie?"

109

Harriet pointed in the opposite direction down the hallway. "She went the back way to the design studio."

"Why?"

Harriet elfishly grinned. "She took a play out of your game book and went to eavesdrop on Jones' and Gary's conversation."

Chapter Eighteen

I tiptoed next to Queenie and whispered in her ear. "Did I miss anything important?"

She whispered back, "No. So far, Jones asked the same questions as the first time." She shrugged. "Maybe he's trying to catch Gary in a lie." I grazed a shushing finger across my lips as she giggled, "Since the cop hasn't cuffed him yet, Gary's answers must match the ones from the last time Jones asked them."

I whispered for her to skedaddle before we got caught. Queenie nodded and headed back to our office. I angled my head perpendicular to the door to see into the studio and not seen. Gary and Jones sat across from one another at Gary's design work table.

Gary pointed to the clock on the wall and pursed his lips. "Detective Jones, I'm on a deadline to get our sample lines complete and don't have time to go over the same questions I answered the first time you asked them. If your goal is trying to trip me up and see if I lied, by now you've checked my responses and got your answer. I told you the truth." Gary stood up. "If you have nothing else, please excuse me. If we're going to get our lines completed in time for our upcoming markets, I have a ton of samples to approve."

Jones stuck his hand into the inside pocket of his suit jacket and pulled out his badge. "Mr. Burkett, let me explain how police interviews work. *I* decide which questions to ask and how many times to ask them, *not you*. *I* decide where and when the interviews take place and how long they last, *not you*. I gave you the courtesy of interviewing you here at your place of work for *your* convenience, not mine. If you don't sit down and behave, we will continue this interview at the precinct. Does me no never mind. Your choice. One thing you better count on is this interview is far from over."

Gary gulped and took his seat.

Jones flipped to a page in his notebook and glared at Gary. "Mr. Burkett, we have a problem."

Gary narrowed his eyes. "What sort of problem?"

"A big one. Your answers have been less than forthcoming."

Gary snapped, "Regarding?"

"For starters, the end of your tenure at Ms. Waxman's company."

Gary reared back and snarled angry as a junkyard dog. "What the hell are you talking about? I told you *the truth*. Leni and I had a difference of opinion as to how to design the line. She fired me and hired someone more in line with her design vision."

Jones cocked a brow. "Be that as it may, your parting was hardly the amicable split you described it to be."

Gary furrowed his brow. "I don't understand why you'd say that. It was her company and her prerogative to fire and hire whoever she wanted to. I accepted the severance amount offered and filed for the unemployment benefits I was entitled to. I didn't challenge the dismissal with the state or fight it anywhere else. I didn't bad mouth her or her company to anyone in the industry."

Jones clucked his tongue. "Mr. Burkett, don't play me for a fool. You failed to disclose Ms. Waxman accused you of stealing her designs before you left."

Gary jutted his jaw. "Not only is it an insult. It's a filthy lie." Gary scoffed. "And it makes no sense. If she fired me because I didn't agree with her design plan, why would I steal her designs?"

Jones arched a brow. "Who says they were *her* designs? The likelier scenario? You stole *your* designs— the ones *you* created while working for Ms. Waxman. Ones *she* rejected." Jones pursed his lips. "As long as you designed them *while working for her*, whether she chose to use them or not is beside the point. Just because you designed them, doesn't mean they were your property to take. They belonged to Ms. Waxman to use or toss in the trash."

Gary funneled his lips. "I left the Rapido building for the last time carrying only my personal belongings in a cardboard box that a company security guard examined and cleared." He waved an arm around the design studio. "Feel free to take a look for yourself."

Jones grunted and moved on. "You also neglected to reveal after you left her company Ms. Waxman blackballed you in the competitive swimwear industry." Jones glared at Gary. "Isn't it a fact, Mr. Burkett, despite several interviews, *not a single one* of Ms. Waxman's competitors offered you a job?"

Gary nodded. "You are right. I didn't find a job in the competitive swimwear market, however, her supposedly blackballing me in the industry isn't the reason. The reason no vendor in the category hired me was *bad timing*. The competitive swimwear industry works way in advance and as such, by that time every vendor was well into the design part of the season. All the vendors in the category were already fully staffed in the design department and didn't need another designer."

Jones cocked a brow. "Then you were probably unemployed for months, possibly a year. Even with unemployment benefits, it must have been a terrible strain to support yourself over such a long time on the severance you received. I bet you were furious at Ms. Waxman for firing you since she knew only too well it would be impossible for you to land another job." Jones leaned forward into Gary's space and bared his teeth. "*Were you, Mr. Burkett? So furious the anger smoldered over the years and you wanted revenge?*"

Jones' notebook made an intimidating *thwack* against the design table as the detective slammed it down. Gary flinched as though he'd been struck "*Well, Mr. Burkett?*"

Gary wisely waited a few beats before answering and kept his cool. "As it turned out, I wasn't out of work long at all. Fortunately, a friend of a professor of mine at design school is a fashion swimwear manufacturer and needed a designer. The owner interviewed me and hired me on the spot." Gary pointed to the black six-button phone on the design table. "Call Stan Herman at Pagoda Swimwear and check it out." Gary smiled. "If anything, I am grateful to Leni for letting me go."

Jones gave Gary a curious look. "Meaning?"

Gary swept an arm behind the work table to the wall covered by his design awards. "Meaning that if Leni didn't fire me, I would not be in the fashion end of the swimwear business where my career took off big time."

Jones leaned forward. "Your problems with Ms. Waxman continued long after you two parted company, didn't they Mr. Burkett? As a matter of fact, they continued right up until the night of her death. Not only did you and Ms. Waxman get into a confrontation, you also made disparaging comments about her at the party."

Jones didn't give Gary a chance to answer. "The fact is Mr. Burkett, Ms. Waxman made it virtually impossible for you to launch your new line. She prevented you from receiving your sample yardage or making production fabric purchases by threatening suppliers to withdraw her business if they shipped you. And at the party, she enraged you by rubbing your nose in it in front of industry colleagues." Jones slammed his fist on the design table. "While making the rounds to greet her guests, she *specifically* stopped at *your table* and taunted you in front of your colleagues at the party. *Didn't she Mr. Burkett? Didn't she?*"

Gary nodded. "She certainly tried. Rest assured, we wouldn't allow *her or any competitor* to control the fate of our business. Only our *customers* earned the right. We made alternate arrangements with several of our key suppliers Leni didn't use and our new line will launch on time."

Jones jotted a couple of lines in his notebook and looked down his nose at Gary. "You were in the ballroom the night of the party *alone* for at least an hour before the party began. How do you explain the security guard allowed you, a guest, not a worker, into the ballroom before the party began?"

Gary clasped his hands together and rested them on the table. "My partner was going to be late due to a work issue and said he would meet me at the mart ballroom. I originally planned to go early and hang out down at the bar on the second floor of the mart. My plans changed after my sister called and said her son graduated from chef school and was recently hired by the catering company providing the meals at the party, and my nephew was part of the party prep team. My nephew got permission from the head chef for me to come into the kitchen at the back of the ballroom. I visited my nephew as well as watched the meal preparations."

Jones said, "How long did you stay in the kitchen?" Jones waved his index finger under Gary's nose. "Remember, Mr. Burkett, this information is easy to confirm…"

Gary ignored the detective's admonition and crunched his eyes in concentration. "Around a half hour."

"Why did you stay in the ballroom alone and not go to the bar downstairs in the mart as you'd originally planned after you completed the kitchen visit?"

Gary tapped his index finger to the side of his head. "By the time I'd get down to the crowded bar and order a drink it would be time to come back to the ballroom." Gary jutted his chin. "By the way, after my kitchen visit, I wasn't alone in the ballroom the whole time."

Jones looked up from his notebook. "Your partner arrived early?"

Gary shook his head. "No. When I came out of the kitchen and went into the ballroom, I ran into an industry colleague there."

"Who?"

Gary said, "*Sharon Hancock.*"

"Why was she in the ballroom?"

Gary shrugged. "No clue."

"You didn't ask?"

Gary looked at Jones strangely. "No. Why would I?"

Jones smirked. "You have no sense of curiosity, Mr. Burkett. You'd make a lousy detective."

Good to know, Columbo.

Jones poised his pen. "What was she doing?"

"Twirling the dreidel." Jones furrowed his brow and Gary laughed, "Maybe she was practicing to win the dreidel contest."

"So, you two were alone in the ballroom together until the party began?"

Gary shook his head. "No. I startled Sharon when I walked in on her. She dropped the dreidel like it was a hot poker and left the ballroom after we exchanged greetings. I was alone in the ballroom until the doors opened half an hour later."

Jones waved his index finger again. "We can check this out too, Mr. Burkett."

Gary held out his hands. "I've no reason to lie."

"So, what did you do all by yourself for so much time?"

Gary shrugged. "Nothing Earth-shattering. Found our table. Checked emails on my phone."

Jones sneered. "That's not all you did, Mr. Burkett. Your fingerprints are on the menorah and dreidel."

How'd they get a match on his fingerprints? As far as I know, Gary was never in trouble with the law...although it would never occur to me to ask.

As if he read my mind, Jones said, "We have your fingerprints to compare to from the Rapido Human Resources Director, so don't try to deny it."

Gary snapped his fingers. "Oh, sorry. Yes, of course. I forgot. I took a look at them both."

Jones smirked. "Why? Planning to convert to Judaism?"

Gary rolled his eyes. "No. For many years my mother was the executive secretary to a Rabbi while I was growing up. I spent a lot of time at the Synagogue she worked at and always enjoyed the Hanukkah parties the temple put on." Gary smiled. "The menorah and dreidel brought back fond memories of my childhood."

Jones closed his notebook and put it in his inside jacket pocket along with his badge. "Those are all my questions for today." Jones smiled coldly. "Don't make any plans to go out of town, Mr. Burkett."

Chapter Nineteen

Three Days Later

I distributed the coffee to the Yentas and surveyed the table. "Boy, I have a story for you guys."

The Yentas gave me a universally reluctant look.

I ignored their annoying response and continued telling my tale. "I sat in Sue Ellen's outer office yesterday afternoon waiting to be called into the inner sanctum. The Princess of Promptness remarkably *kept me waiting* for almost ten minutes. Her door was partially opened, so I took a peek inside to see whose meeting ran over time. None other than Allen Brown from Winner's Circle Competitive Swimwear." I widened my eyes. "You'll never believe who was with him—*Sharon Hancock*!"

Joan pursed her lips. "Wasn't she arrested for flashing?"

I nodded. "She was." I held my hands out in contrition. "I apologize. I forgot to tell you guys I spoke to my cousin Janie a few days ago. If you remember, Janie's a nurse at the hospital where Sharon was brought to on Christmas Eve. Janie is also a friend of Sharon's from their nursing school days. Sharon is out on bail. My cousin posted the bond." I sighed and crossed my fingers. "Janie's a decent, trusting person. I hope she doesn't get burned."

Sonia gave me the big eyes. "Sharon was with

Allen? How weird."

I asked, "Why? They sat together at Leni's party. Maybe they struck a deal and she's working for him."

Sonia stroked her chin and mused aloud. "Well, *now* I understand why…"

Hope asked, "What do you understand why now?"

Sonia said, "If she is working for Allen, it hasn't been for long. Last Tuesday my sister and I were eating lunch at The Blue China Moon. Sharon, Hadassah Waxman, and her brother were sitting together only two tables from ours. The three of them were going over a set of documents. I couldn't hear the conversation, but it looked as if the three of them were working together."

Queenie nodded. "You might be onto something. Hadassah didn't agree with a lot of Leni's decisions—including firing Sharon."

Hope funneled her lips. "Well, if Allen and Sharon worked together, then any opportunity for Sharon to return to Rapido must have fallen through."

Joan asked, "Is Winner's Circle part of the competitive swimwear matrix at Bainbridge?"

I shook my head. "No. Since Allied was new to the category and unfamiliar with the vendors, Leni Waxman advised the company on which four competitive swimwear vendors to buy from. Leni and Allen battled each other in a courtroom, so Leni didn't recommend Winner's Circle as one of the four suppliers."

Joan smirked, "From the sound of the retail disaster competitive swimwear has been for Allied, Leni did Allen a favor."

Sonia winked. "Considering the volume of Sue Ellen's crabbing about her store having the worst sell-through of competitive swimwear in the entire Allied chain if Leni wasn't already dead, I'm pretty sure the Queen of Mean would be ready, willing, and able to do the deed."

Joan mused, "It's a wonder Allied hasn't dropped the category by now."

Always practical Sonia waved an index finger in the air. "Nah. They've invested too much time and space to drop it—at least, not yet. Allied chomped at the bit for the opportunity to take more of the competitive swimwear business away from sporting goods stores. Believe me, Allied will come out of the mess fine. To hit their department profitability margin requirements, Allied will squeeze every last drop of markdown money from those four suppliers to make up the shortfall. Whoever doesn't pony up enough will be out of the stores."

Queenie tapped her index finger on the tip of her nose. "So, if Winner's Circle is not part of the matrix, what were Allen and Sharon doing at Bainbridge?"

I grinned. "Trying to bury Rapido in the same grave as Leni Waxman."

Hope asked, "How?"

I said, "From the sound of the conversation, Allied revamped the way the category style selections will be chosen and orders placed. They took all style selections away from vendors and formed a buying committee from their retail divisions to review the lines and choose the styles. Since she is the most senior swimwear buyer and has the biggest volume department in their chain, Allied appointed Sue Ellen as the head of the committee. Allied also opened the door for other vendors to compete. After all the lines are reviewed, the committee will make their final selections in a styleout and all divisions will uniformly have the same styles and colors on their floors."

Queenie said, "So, there's no guarantee any of the four original vendors will make the matrix going forward."

I nodded. "So, it seems. And that's the reason Allen and Sharon took the meeting. They placed the Allied competitive swimwear debacle where it belonged—squarely on Leni's shoulders, and Sue Ellen agreed. Allen and Sharon pitched the concept of throwing Rapido out as the worst-performing line. In addition to giving each vendor individual open-to-buy dollars, Allen and Sharon proposed also dividing Rapido's amongst all the other suppliers—including Winner's Circle."

Sonia arched a brow. "Sounds to me as if those two wannabe vultures wasted no time pecking at Leni's carcass in the hopes of replacing the worst performing retailing competitive swimwear brand at Allied with their line."

Joan pursed her lips. "Or they wanted to finish what they started the night of the party…"

****

After the Yenta coffee klatch, Queenie and I left the mart. We pulled into the double driveway of our factory at the same time and she barely missed hitting a lamppost. My innards twisted around like a slinky as I stared gape-mouthed at the dozen LAPD squad cars blocking the entrance to the building. I followed Queenie's lead as she zig-zagged her way to cut around the cop cars and pulled into her parking slot. As I parked, Gary drove in behind us. I opened the front door of the factory with the same level of caution as the bomb squad defusing an unmarked package.

We found Harriet Cowan in the lobby muttering to herself and walking in a continuous figure-eight. I caught our secretary as she made the turn and blocked her path. "Harriet, why are the police here?"

Harriet wrung her hands. "Detective Jones and an army of uniforms marched in at seven-forty-five this morning."

I smirked, "I'm gonna take a wild guess they're not here to collect donations for the policeman's charity ball."

Harriet said, "The detective waved a search warrant, itching to serve it."

Queenie turned to Harriet. "Who did they serve the warrant to?"

Harriet pointed to the three of us. "The detective *wanted* to serve the warrant to one of you. The only employees in the building were our receptionist-Monica, the sample sewers, the production and warehouse crews, and me. As the most senior one available, I got the honors."

Queenie said, "What are they looking for?"

Harriet turned her head and the bleached blonde platinum hair teased into a poufy bouffant shifted from side to side. "I dunno. The warrant didn't list anything specific."

Gary clutched his chest and whispered, "Are they here to *arrest* someone?"

Harriet gulped. "No. At least not yet. The warrant is a blanket court order giving the police the authority to search the facility and confiscate anything they deemed questionable..."

I asked, "Twelve patrol cars are outside. How many police are in the building?"

Harriet counted on her fingers. "Four uniforms in the executive and design wings and eight in the warehouse."

I glanced at my watch. Ten on the nose. At this rate, the search could last all day. Unbelievable. "Will they let us go into our offices?"

Harriet shook her head. "Nope. The detective made it clear the search encompassed the *entire* campus. The detective made me announce on the PA for all employees to enter the lunchroom until the police completed their search. They searched my office first and made Monica move while they searched the reception desk. They cleared the two of us, and we're the only ones exempt from waiting in the lunchroom."

Our factory is a substantial-sized building. And the warehouse attached to it occupies an entire city block. Between the production and distribution teams, over one hundred employees worked in the warehouse. The lunchroom is a huge room, but it isn't big enough to accommodate all the employees at the same time.

I snorted. "And Detective Jones expected *all* our employees to fit into the lunchroom at the same time?"

Harriet laughed. "He did until I brought the detective to the lunchroom to see for himself that it wouldn't accommodate us all at once. We sent all the warehouse workers outside on the loading dock and the factory personnel to the lunchroom. It's crowded but it'll work."

Holy guacamole. "Did the detective say how long this is gonna take?"

Harriet clucked her tongue. "Nope. They'll inform us when they're finished. Do me a favor. Get down to the lunch room. Seeing the company senior execs sitting in the lunch room will help calm the nerves of the crowd. Make sure enough coffee is brewed, so the natives don't get too restless."

Normally a hotbed of gossip and gab, the packed to-maximum-capacity Mermaid lunchroom was eerily quiet as a church during Sunday services. The only sound? The percolating third pot of fresh coffee I'd brewed. The tension exacerbated by the fear of a murder investigation was thick enough to cut with a dull knife. Mostly heads down, the group kept to themselves. I glanced around and took the temperature of the crowd. Red hot. I checked the time and the supply of coffee. We almost ran out of both.

As though he read my mind, Detective Jones's massive body filled the entrance to the lunchroom. All conversations halted as every head in the room turned and faced the cop.

Jones said, "Our search of the premises is complete. We appreciate your patience and cooperation. You're all free to go back to your work areas." The crowd stood and made a mass exodus for the door, then Jones blocked the way out. The cop put out a hand. "I'm sorry. Let me revise my announcement." Jones waved a clear evidence bag like the bait for a mousetrap under Gary's nose. Gary squeezed my hand so tightly it's a wonder my fingers still worked when Jones lasered his eyes at our partner. "All *except* Mr. Burkett."

Chapter Twenty

News of Gary's arrest spread through the swimwear industry with the speed of a wildfire. The phone didn't stop ringing the rest of the day—calls from the press, competitors, customers, and suppliers—all angling for the inside scoop. After a few hours of nonstop interruptions, I instructed the receptionist to switch all the incoming calls over to voicemail.

The next morning, I stopped at the newsstand in front of the mart deli on my way to A Jolt of Java. I pushed through the crowd like a halfback scoring a touchdown and snatched the last copy of the West Coast Apparel News off the kiosk rack. The boldface headline above the fold read *Mermaid Designer Collared for Waxman's Murder*

The Yenta mood was somber as I laid the newspaper in the center of the table.

Joan asked, "You were in the lunchroom when he was arrested?"

I nodded numbly. Gary being shackled by handcuffs is an image forever branded into my memory. "Jones told everyone except Gary they could leave the lunchroom. I followed the rest of the group out and then hung back. The door was propped open, so I stood to the side and eavesdropped. They sat at the table in the back of the lunchroom and couldn't see me. Jones laid the evidence bag on the table."

I surveyed the group. "Jones put on surgical gloves, took out a container of nicotine and an E-cigarette from the evidence bag, and placed them in front of Gary. The detective asked, 'Mr. Burkett, do you smoke or vape?' Gary said no. Jones shoved the nicotine and E-cigarette over to Gary and snarled, 'Then *how* do you explain these two items *buried* in the bottom of your desk drawer?'"

Sonia asked, "Gary gave a plausible explanation?"

I nodded. "Gary explained his partner is the vaper, not him. He told Jones that Ken gave him a spare pack to hold for him in case he ran out of nicotine or if his E-cigarette wore out. Jones didn't buy Gary's story. The detective raised his hands palms-up. 'Stand up and put your hands behind your back, Mr. Burkett. *You're under arrest for the murder of Leni Waxman.*' I shuddered at the sound of the clink as Jones cuffed Gary and read him his rights."

I grimaced. "Jones stood behind Gary as they walked to the lunchroom door. I walked in front of them and blocked the way. I didn't care if I pissed the cop off or not. I ignored Jones and looked Gary in the eye. I said, Do. Not. Say. Another. Word. Do. You. Hear. Me? No matter what he says or asks, do not respond. No matter what he does, do not react. Your lawyer will meet you at the station. Gary's eyes were as big as coasters from fear as he nodded his understanding. I stepped aside to let the detective perp-walk Gary through the factory."

Sonia asked, "Is Ms. Markowitz representing Gary?"

I smiled. "Of course—who else?"

Joan asked, "You saw Ms. M.?"

I nodded. "Yes. I went to her office after she met

with Gary."

Sonia's concerned eyes searched mine. "How is Gary?"

Hope wrung her hands. "Poor guy. He must be terrified."

I grinned. "Ms. M. said he complained about the scratchy prison jumpsuit fabric irritating his sensitive skin and he hated the tacky bright orange color because it washed him out."

Queenie clucked her tongue. "It better be only his nerves talking. Because Detective Jones isn't kidding around."

I nodded. "Believe me, Gary realizes how much trouble he is in. Ms. M. said Jones had enough evidence to arrest Gary, but it was all circumstantial. Jones has no smoking gun."

Sonia stroked her fingertips across her chin. "She's right. Jones can't prove it is nicotine from the *specific jar in Gary's desk drawer* used to poison Leni."

Hope scrunched her nose. "Nonetheless, *Gary's fingerprints* are on the dreidel and the nicotine jar found *hidden* in *his desk drawer*." She flexed her index fingers. "It's not a big stretch to say one plus one equals two."

Joan bit her lip. "True. And if it's a motive Jones is focusing on, unfortunately, Gary fills the bill."

I furrowed my brow. "He's not the only one. So do a lot of others."

Hope pointed a spoon at Queenie. "The homicide cops on TV always say…?"

Queenie and I chorused, "*Follow the money*."

Sonia waved ta-da. "In that case, we have a suspect cast of thousands."

I said, "If you tack on who had the *most to lose*, my

money is still on Sharon Hancock. Leni wasn't satisfied just *firing* Sharon. Leni made it her business to *ruin* Sharon's life."

Gary Burkett is no more a murderer than Queenie or me. *Eventually*, Detective Jones will *probably* pull his massive head out of his ass and come to the same conclusion. However, I'm not one to leave anything to chance.

I glanced around the table. "Jones needs a second set of eyes to crack this case—whether he realizes it or not. And yours truly is the one to supply them. Now, all I've gotta do is put my peepers to work and prove Sharon is the culprit."

I snapped my fingers and laughed. "No biggie. Piece of cake."

The Yentas groaned in unison.

Thanks a lot, ladies.

Your support is underwhelming.

Chapter Twenty-One

There is never a *good time* to be incarcerated, especially for a crime you weren't guilty of committing, but as the head designer of our company, the timing of Gary's arrest could not be worse for Mermaid Swimwear. We are in a single seasonal business. There is no margin for error and if you snooze you lose.

The only plausible thing to do? Divide up the responsibilities we normally share. Queenie would focus on finance and production while I concentrated on design and sales.

Mira Kumar, our cover-up and newly-created competitive swimwear designer, and I met in the design studio to bring me up to speed on the completion of our new lines. After we went through all the line lists, I breathed a little easier. The good news? All of our established product lines were complete and ready for the upcoming trade shows. The bad news? So far, we've only received half of the competitive swimwear sample yardage from our Asian suppliers. While the quality is excellent and their costs phenomenally low, these factories are the ones we use for our private-label products and have longer turnaround times. They are not accustomed to the shorter ones our branded divisions require.

Mira wrung her hands in frustration as she studied the huge work-in-progress calendar on the wall behind her design table. "We've received around half of our orders. Six of the shipments that have landed are stuck in customs for a secondary inspection. As of today, no pending release date has been given. The balance hasn't left Asia yet. At the rate the sample yardage is coming in, even if they air in all the remaining open goods, we're going to miss three important milestones in two weeks." She waved the purchase orders in the air like a flag of surrender. "If the yardage comes in perfect and the sample sewers work twelve hours a day, considering the number of styles left to cut and sew, the line will still be incomplete for the New York market."

I said, "If you remember, the *only reason* we went to our Asian suppliers in the first place is because *Leni Waxman* put the kibosh on our domestic vendor orders. Well, Leni is now out of the picture and it's time to circle back to Plan A." I pointed to the phone on the table. "Call Elena Sosa at Stretch America Textiles, Ricky Greenblatt at Gifford, as well as all the other suppliers we use, and make as many appointments as possible for tomorrow. We'll take the swatches of the patterns we're still missing from our original orders and see how close we get to them using either in-stock prints or ones that have existing screens that can be printed and delivered in a week. I bet we come close. And if the yardage arrives from Asia, we hold the prints in case we need to add more groups to the line."

****

Mira worked miracles and scheduled us for two-hour back-to-back meetings starting at eight in the morning. We conducted a nonstop merry-go-round of meetings—no time for a potty stop, let alone a meal break. The good news? We found suitable patterns of in-stock yardage shippable on the same day. If these vendors perform as promised we will complete the new line on time.

Or maybe I spoke too soon…We walked out of Elena Sosa's showroom carrying two armfuls of pattern headers and order copies just as *Hadassah Waxman* opened the door. Mira and I looked at one another and Yankee baseball legend Yogi Berra's famous line "It's déjà vu all over again." played inside my head.

I'd starve earning a living as a poker player. Hadassah took a gander at my kisser and burst out laughing. All things considered, this was a far better reaction than as my dad says, a poke in the nose using a sharp stick.

Hadassah grinned and offered me her right hand. I stuck mine out as timidly as though sticking a toe into a pool of ice water. Then she pointed to the print headers in my hand. "Are you coming or going?"

Why? Was she planning to pick up where Leni left off?

I angled my head toward the exit. "Going."

Hadassah asked, "To another appointment?"

I shook my head. "Nope. This is our last one. Why?"

Hadassah held up a folder. "I'm only dropping off some lab dip color approvals here. It won't take more than a couple of minutes. If you don't mind waiting for me, are you up to grabbing a coffee?"

They say curiosity killed the cat, but that didn't stop me from accepting the invitation.

Mira took the headers out of my hands. "I'll drop everything off at the factory and then call it a day."

****

Twenty minutes later Hadassah and I took our

beverages to the back of Sam's, a greasy spoon coffee shop a few blocks from the mart. We sat at a scarred Formica table yellowed by age. As we sipped our coffees we made small talk.

I pointed to the blood-red rose behind her ear. "I noticed you and your mother both wore red roses at the Hanukkah party. Family tradition or do you both just love the flowers?"

Hadassah patted her hair and smiled. "A little bit of both, I guess. Believe it or not, my tough-as-nails mother had a softer side. She was an avid gardener. She loved beautiful flowers and red roses were her passion." Hadassah laughed. "Of course, Mom was famous for taking her daily frustrations out on weeds by swinging a vicious hoe. And the stubborn ones? She drenched them in weed killer. By the time I learned to walk, I hoed, raked, and planted in her garden. I inherited her green thumb and love of red roses. I've gardened my entire life."

An interesting but not particularly useful insight into the Waxman women. To avoid making this cozy coffee klatch a total waste of time, I took the bull by the horns to get some information.

I studied her over the rim of my coffee cup. "The word out on the street is you've made a lot of changes at Rapido."

Hadassah nodded and laughed. "My mother is probably rolling over in her grave by now."

I arched a brow. "Making a statement or a change in the corporate course?"

Hadassah pursed her lips. "My mother was a control freak whose corporate philosophy was her way or the highway. Let's just say I made it clear to her that I didn't approve of the way she ran the company. Now that I am *finally* able to change it, I am."

Whoa.

Never one to squander an opportunity, I poked the stick. "So, I guess you were shocked by Gary's arrest for Leni's murder…"

Hadassah drew her lips into a thin line of disapproval. "My mother *never* took ownership of *anything*, despite realizing she screwed up royally by not allowing Gary to make needed design changes." Hadassah's eyes turned hard as diamonds. "Leni Waxman was a ruthless tyrant who *destroyed anyone or anything* standing in her way. I wasn't shocked Gary did it. They say revenge is best served cold. My only surprise is that it took him so long to serve his."

I blinked my surprise. "You've known the guy since your high school days. You *really* believe he's capable of *murder*?"

Her tongue clucked with righteous indignation. "What *I* believe is not important. What *the police* believe is. Since *they* believe Gary is the killer, why shouldn't *I*?"

I gave her the big eyes. "Your mother made her share of enemies who had much bigger bones to pick with her than Gary. The chatter in the industry is that the list of who Leni tried to destroy is as long as your arm." I ticked off a short list on my fingers. "For starters, Allen Brown— he developed a fabric that adds speed to a swimmer by repelling water off a swimsuit and says Leni stole the idea. Elena Sosa—Rapido is Elena's biggest client. If Leni followed through on her threat to cancel all her orders if Elena did business with Mermaid, SAT would be out of business. And my personal pick—

Sharon Hancock—Leni not only fired Sharon she ruined her career."

Hadassah smirked. "Allen's fabric innovation—so far, in a court of law, he's failed to prove it anything more than a fabrication of his imagination. As for Elena—if she spent more time developing a wider customer base and less time competing at Martial Arts meets, she could have called my mother's bluff and told her to pound sand. My mother was a bully who loved to push people around because they allowed her to intimidate them. If someone pushed her back, she'd fold like a cheap card table."

"And Sharon Hancock?"

Hadassah's face clouded over. "I'm trying to right my mother's wrong. I've presented Sharon with an offer to come back to Rapido. Sharon is going over the contract details now with her lawyer. Barring any complications, we'll finalize the deal by the end of this week."

Barring any complications? Ha! I've got a news flash for you. Share it with Hadassah or let her find out herself? Nana's voice reverberated inside my head. "Always speak your mind."

I looked Hadassah Waxman in the eye. "A nice gesture on your part, however, the ship has already sailed."

Hadassah snapped like a cranky Croc. "*Meaning what*?"

"Meaning I overheard Sharon and Allen *together* in Sue Ellen Magee's office a few days ago pitching the idea of Allied booting Rapido off the corporate vendor matrix and substituting it with Winner's Circle."

Hadassah shrugged and made an '*I'm done*' motion

with a wipe-away flick of a wrist. "Pity. I gave her far more credit for brains. *She will live to regret her decision.*" She smirked. "*Anyone else* on your supposed suspect list?"

Leni Waxman's darling daughter inhaled a sharp breath when I smiled sweetly and saluted her with my coffee cup. "We certainly can't leave *you* off the list now, can we?"

Chapter Twenty-Two

I related my coffee klatch with Hadassah Waxman to the Yentas the following morning.

Queenie tapped her index finger on the tip of her nose. "You may be onto something with Leni's daughter as the killer."

I made a sour face. "Nah, she pissed me off with her BS reason for accepting Gary as the murderer. I only threw it out to ruffle her feathers."

Sonia rubbed her chin. "I dunno, Hol. If you remember, at the reception after Leni's funeral, Hadassah raised quite a ruckus regarding *the length of time* it took your pal the coroner to release Leni's body."

Hope nodded. "Sonia is right. She didn't shut up about it."

Joan arched a brow. "Maybe Hadassah had a damned good reason to plant Leni's body six feet under ASAP."

I wagged my index finger. "If the family wasn't *Jewish*, I'd be suspicious something nefarious was afoot."

Joan asked, "What difference does it make if the family is Jewish?"

Queenie said, "Because we bury our dead quickly. Jewish law says unless someone dies on the Sabbath, the body must be buried in a plain pine coffin *the day after the death*. We mourn for one week and then go on with our lives as both Jewish law dictates and how our late loved one expects us to do."

I said, "The reason Hadassah got so upset is because the family could not conduct their mourning on a timely basis. As to who murdered Leni? My money is still on Sharon. Leni tried her best to destroy Sharon's career. Thanks to Leni's relentlessness, Sharon's personal life unraveled too. Sharon had nothing left to lose and payback is a bitch. First Sharon killed Leni and now she's trying to bury Rapido along with the company founder."

Hope funneled her lips. "A good theory. How are you going to prove it?"

I tapped my lower lip. "I'll get back to you on it."

****

Two Nights Later

Six thirty on the nose. Queenie's weekly Pilates class ought to be finished soon, so I parked and went into Coast Burgers to get a table before the popular joint filled up. The hostess guided me to a booth for two in the center of the main dining room. I slid into the side facing the front and made a one-eighty to spot Queenie—no such luck.

I turned a quarter of the way right and locked eyes with Sharon Hancock. She sat dwarfed in a huge family-sized booth two over from me facing the entrance. She fidgeted as she anxiously checked her watch and looked at the front door. I tried not to react as she took an *e-cigarette* out of her purse and fiddled around with it. The grayish complexion, the downcast curve of her lips, and the dark circles under her eyes—the woman looked like overcooked crap. I slapped a sincere-looking smile on my kisser and waved hello. She finger-waved a half-hearted return to my greeting and glanced at the reception desk.

Serendipity? You bet your sweet ass. I prayed for Queenie to run late as I moseyed over to Sharon's table and without asking permission, slid into the seat across from her.

I beamed a hundred-thousand-watt-smile. I clasped my pinkies together and held up my hands. "Pinky swear," I giggled, "I'm not following you."

Sharon laughed sardonically. "Well, there's a relief."

Trust me, I would if I could.

Sharon cocked a brow when I asked, "So, your Sue Ellen meeting went well?" I smiled sheepishly. "It's not that I *meant* to eavesdrop on your meeting—it's just that her office door was open and I sat only a few feet away in her outer office waiting my turn. So, I couldn't help hearing the conversation."

Sharon shrugged. "How did it go? Hard to say. You know how it is. Buyers don't commit to anything. She didn't say yes to our proposal but she didn't say no either." Sharon smiled evilly. "One thing is certain—if *any competitive* swimwear vendor gets the boot, and Sue Ellen has any sway, *Rapido is toast*. I'd say it's a good bet Allied Stores drops Rapido and Winner's Circle and your new line will be added to the Allied vendor matrix."

I asked, "When did you start working for Allen?"

"A week before the Hanukkah party."

"No kidding."

Sharon pursed her lips. "Surprised Leni didn't screw it up for me?"

I wrinkled my brow. "Not exactly."

She made a sour face. "So, spit it out."

"If you were already working for Allen by the time of the party, why didn't either you or Allen say so when Leni harassed you both?"

Sharon jutted her chin. "One—It was none of her damned business. Two—We have a major kickoff program prepared for the New York market at the end of this month and plan to officially announce my joining the company to the industry then."

I tipped my head the same way Siggie does when he tries to understand. "I'm confused. If you've been working for Allen since before the party, why did my colleague Sonia Wilson see you not long ago at The Blue China Moon, sitting across from Hadassah Waxman and her brother? According to Sonia, the three of you were going over a set of documents like an employment contract."

Sharon's voice rose several octaves and squeaked in righteous indignation. "*Hadassah reached out to me, not the other way around.* She said she wanted to right her mother's wrong. She asked for the meeting to present her idea." Sharon shrugged. "I figured why not? No one gets cancer from having a conversation."

I scrunched my nose. "If documents were prepared, things moved from the discussion stage into the take action stage—at least from the Waxman's perspective." I smirked. "I bet my boat you neglected to tell them you'd been working for Allen since before the party."

Sharon clucked her tongue. "*Why the hell would I do that?*"

That she asked the question spoke legions.

I leaned forward and went in for the kill. "So, maybe you were never serious regarding her offer. Maybe you told Allen beforehand about the proposed Waxman meeting and he urged you to hear them out and spy for him at the same time."

Sharon glared at me through steely eyes. "And what if I did? A *Waxman is a Waxman.* And trust me, the apple didn't fall far from the tree."

Right as rain, in my opinion. As for me confirming it? On the second Tuesday of next week. Sharon Hancock did not earn my respect—only my increased distrust and disdain.

I gleaned everything possible from the hot topic and changed the subject to, if nothing else, lower the temperature at the table.

"Funny, I've never run into you in this neck of the woods before. Do you live at the beach?"

She curled her upper lip and spat, "Hardly. Thanks to *Leni and my ex*, the beach is too rich for my blood."

So much for lowering the temperature. Undaunted, I soldiered on.

"Where do you live?"

She blushed and cast her eyes down. "I moved a week ago from Palms to the other side of town. I rent a studio apartment over a garage from a friend who has a bungalow in West Hollywood above the Sunset Strip."

I waved an arm around the dining room. "Coast Burgers is a chain. There is a location not far from where you live. It's next to Hollywood Medical Center Hospital where my cousin works as an emergency nurse. I live here in the marina. But I go to the Hollywood Coast Burgers location often because I meet my cousin Janie there for lunch twice a month."

Sharon widened her eyes. "What's your cousin's last name?"

"Goldberg. Why?"

Sharon slapped her cheeks. "You've gotta be kidding. The friend I rent the apartment from? She's an emergency nurse on staff at that hospital named *Jane Goldberg*. We've been friends for a long time. She's the Godmother to my children. Must be the same woman." Sharon made an hourglass outline with her fingers. "Busty and a flat-as-a-pancake ass. Short—an inch or two taller than you. Green eyes. Mid-length brown curly hair." Sharon touched her face. "Strawberry beauty mark on the right side of her chin."

Whoa. She described my cousin exactly. I spoke to Janie a few days ago. Funny she never said a word about her new tenant. Hmm.

I struggled to keep a poker face. "Yep, that's Janie all right. Such a small world. Did you grow up in the valley? Janie and I went to Grant High together. We're around the same age as you. I'm sorry. If you went to Grant, I don't remember you."

Sharon scrunched her nose. "No, I grew up in the South Bay."

"So how do you know Janie?"

Sharon smiled. "We went through the UCLA nursing school program together."

I batted my eyes. "*You're a nurse*? So, why are you selling swimwear?" I wrinkled my nose and joked, "Discover you can't stand the sight of blood?"

Sharon smiled sadly. "I didn't graduate. I got married and dropped out of the nursing program my senior year to put my husband through law school."

I tapped the menu in front of her and arched a brow. "This is a long drive for a burger when the same one is available practically in your backyard."

Sharon sighed. "Not that I owe you an explanation for where I choose to eat, but I came to this location to see my children. They live with their father in Playa del Rey. He's bringing the kids here." Sharon's eyes filled. "He not only has full custody; he convinced the court to rule I can only see my children for a few hours twice a month with *supervised visitation*."

Call me crazy—I bet your pesky flashing habit might be the reason...

Sharon glanced at the restaurant entrance and her face lit up bright as a Christmas tree. She pointed the e-cigarette at the reception desk. "Please excuse me. My children are here." She looked at the e-cigarette clamped tightly in her fist as if it appeared on its own and panicked. "Oh my God! I better get rid of this and fast." She opened her purse and threw the e-cigarette in. "If my ex sees I'm still vaping, he'll use it as another flim-flam *I am a bad influence on the children* excuse to prevent me from seeing them all together."

After Sharon made the introduction, I squeezed out of the booth and barely avoided colliding with an adorable set of elementary school-aged children—a boy and a girl who squealed, "*Mommy!*" as they ran into Sharon's open arms.

Chapter Twenty-Three

I filled in the Yentas regarding my Sharon Hancock encounter and hoisted my coffee cup to toast Queenie. "If Queenie's Pilates class didn't run late, I'd still be in the dark about so many things. Since speaking to Sharon, I am more convinced than ever that she murdered Leni."

I counted the reasons on my fingers. "*Motive*—Leni fired Sharon for no good cause and made it her business to blackball her in the industry. Then to put the final nail in Sharon's coffin, Leni told Sharon's husband about the flashing and Sharon lost custody of her children. *Means*—Sharon went to nursing school. She knows which poisons are most effective and the best way to apply them for maximum damage. And since Sharon vapes, she has access to nicotine. *Opportunity*—Sharon was alone in the ballroom the night of the party before it began. Gary entered the ballroom and observed Sharon *monkeying around with the dreidel*. She ran out of the ballroom as if her hair caught on fire when she encountered Gary." I snapped my fingers. "I'd say it's game-set-match."

Joan snarked, "It's a wonder you didn't make a citizen's arrest."

Queenie poked her index finger into her cleavage. "If I didn't show up, I bet she would...or Goddess help us, do something *even crazier*."

Dang—such a great idea. Too bad it didn't occur to

me last night.

I huffed, "*In front of her children*? Hardly. Instead, I called Ms. M. and gave her the lowdown. Ms. M. and Detective Jones go way back. Hopefully, she can bang some sense into his thick skull and get him to arrest the right suspect. I also called my cousin Janie. I am meeting her for lunch tomorrow. That she somehow neglected to mention *Sharon* is her new tenant is beyond me."

****

The next morning, I left Siggie at my dock neighbor Muriel Lobowsky's boat for their weekly play day and then headed downtown. I pulled into the left turn lane at the intersection of Admiralty Way and Lincoln Blvd. The light turned green and I accelerated. I tried to complete the turn, and it took a herculean effort using every ounce of arm strength and both hands to move the steering wheel a mere quarter of the way. Huh? The car limped into the turn and I signaled to get into the right lane and onto the eastbound 90 Freeway. Good luck, Schlivnik. Rush hour in the marina. A legion of impatient drivers not in a conciliatory mood sat behind the wheels of wall-to-wall cars. At last, a good Samaritan waved me in, but my steering wheel didn't budge. I flipped on the emergency blinkers and braced myself for either a rear-end accident or if I got lucky, only a symphony of horns and a chorus line of middle finger salutes.

The Auto Club arrived forty-five minutes later. By then, thanks to me, traffic on the northbound side of Lincoln was backed up halfway to LAX. It took an hour to tow the convertible downtown to my mechanic Johnny's garage. Queenie met me at Johnny's and chauffeured me to the mart.

I finished the last of a cup of coffee when my cell phone rang. Caller ID said Johnny on the line. I checked my watch. Hmm…not quite two hours since I left the convertible in Johnny's capable hands. Maybe the issue is something minor. Right. And maybe I have a future as a basketball center.

I pressed the on button and Johnny got right to the point.

"The reason your steering wheel wouldn't budge is because there is no power steering fluid in the reservoir."

I breathed a sigh of relief. "Okay. So, you refilled it, right? Can I come get the car now? If I hustle, I can still make my lunch date on time."

"You might still make it to your lunch date, just not in *your* car."

I looked at the phone kind of wonky. "Good gravy, Johnny how long does it possibly take to refill the reservoir?"

He replied in the same tone of voice to explain the issue to a toddler. "That was the *first thing* we did. The problem is, no sooner did we fill the reservoir than the fluid drained out again."

"So, the reservoir is bad? No surprise. It's an *old* car. Stands to reason the reservoir wore out."

Johnny barked out a laugh. "No such luck. The reservoir is in perfect condition—except for the ten pinpricks somebody poked through it."

My stomach dropped to my toes. "Are you saying the car has been *tampered with*?"

Johnny snorted. "Well, those pinpricks didn't get poked all on their own. You better rent a car. Yours is going to be out of commission for a while."

"Why? How long will it take you to get the part?"

"It's not how long it will take me to get the part. It's how long your car will be at the *police impound garage.* The forensic team will be going over every inch of your car since it is now *evidence of a crime.*" He sighed, "Holly Swimsuit, who did you piss off and what kind of mess did you step into *this time*?"

The protest died in my throat. This was not my first rodeo. Regrettably, Johnny delivered this kind of news way too many times.

Johnny lowered his voice and made his tone ominous. "One of these times, your luck will run out and you and this classic car are not gonna make it out alive." He laughed to soften the blow. "You've gotta cut this crap out. I have two more kids to put through college and I'm counting on you to help finance their educations."

****

Two hours later Miguel Martinez strode into the showroom. Hmm. Bad news travels fast. We had not spoken to or seen one another since the infamous New Year's Eve fiasco. And from his grim expression, a few decades of separation might be too soon. I plastered a *glad-to-see-you smile* on my kisser and hoped for the best.

The last thing I wanted? Miguel Martinez to take me into his arms and whisper. "Thank goodness you weren't hurt...*this time.*"

This time. Here we go again. Another country is heard from. I needed another lecture, especially from *him*, like I needed a bigger tush.

I extricated myself from his embrace and arched a brow. "I should be flattered. A busy man like you dropped *everything* to race over here *just* to get in my face."

Miguel clucked his tongue. "Out of *concern for* you. I wanted to make sure you are okay."

Right, Mickey. And I sprouted wings.

I turned a three-sixty and patted myself down. "Good news. As you see, all my parts are *exactly* where they are supposed to be."

He ignored my demonstration and rubbed his tummy. "I'm starved. Wanna grab a bite? I've got a hankering for the Moo Shoo over at the Blue China Moon."

I shook my head. "I'd love to, but no can do. I've got back-to-back appointments all afternoon, so I ordered lunch. It will be delivered any minute now. Give me a call next time so I can pencil you in."

Miguel's eyes bugged as I ushered him out the door. "I appreciate your concern. Thanks for stopping by."

Chapter Twenty-Four

By the time I sent Miguel packing and put out a few fires, lunchtime became closer to early dinnertime. I called Janie to apologize for standing her up, explained my situation, and asked to reschedule for the next day. Unfortunately, she had twelve-hour shifts the rest of the week and would be unable to leave the hospital. She was off duty over the weekend, so we made arrangements to meet for lunch on Saturday at El Palacio, a landmark Mexican restaurant in the heart of West Hollywood featuring the best Margaritas, guacamole, and chips this side of Guadalajara.

****

We sipped our Margaritas and made small talk while munching on the chips and guacamole. I purposely didn't ask Janie about her new tenant over the phone. I wanted to see her reaction as I sprung the question. Between sips and chips, I eased my way into the subject.

"You'll never guess who I ran into while I waited for Queenie a few nights ago at the *marina location* of Coast Burgers. *Sharon Hancock*, of all people. I asked if she lived in the area. She said no, she lived on the other side of town. She said she moved from Palms to West Hollywood into a studio apartment over a garage from a friend who has a bungalow in West Hollywood above the Sunset Strip. So, I asked her the reason she came to the marina since there is a Coast Burgers in her neighborhood next to the Hollywood Medical Center Hospital. I said I go to the Hollywood Coast location because my cousin Janie is an emergency room nurse at the hospital. Sharon said she only came to the marina to meet her children for dinner. Then Sharon looks at me funny and asks my cousin's last name. She almost fell over when I told her."

I gave Janie the big eyes. "*Wanna know why, Janie?*"

Janie squirmed in her seat. "No. I know why."

I pursed my lips. "You and I are more like sisters than cousins. We always tell one another *everything*—or so I thought. So, why keep Sharon as your tenant a state secret? *Especially from me?*"

Janie hung her head. "I dunno. You're right…It's …"

A bubble of annoyance rose from my gut and accented my tone. "It's *what?*"

Her shoulders slumped. "I let my heart rule over my head and now I'm regretting my decision. And I was too embarrassed to tell you about the bonehead decision I made."

Huh?

"Why do you regret the decision? Sharon's your friend. Your friend was in trouble. You're a decent person and found a way to help your friend out. Why be embarrassed for doing a good deed?"

Janie pinched her brow. "You're right. My intentions were good. But you know what they say— the road to hell is paved with good intentions." Janie's eyes filled. "And the more I learn of her troubles, the more I worry about her."

"What got your alarm clock ringing?"

"Sharon came to my house after she saw her kids the other night."

"Did she say she ran into me?"

Janie shook her head. "No. She was upset and crying. Her ex told her his law firm opened an office in San Diego and he'd been appointed to head it. He and the children are moving to La Jolla at the end of this month."

I said, "He has full custody, but she *does have* parental visitation rights."

Janie tapped her fingers across her cheeks. "Her visitation rights are limited. She has only supervised visitations, so the children are unable to go to her home for a weekend. She can't force the ex to bring the children to LA. If she wants to see them, she will be going to San Diego."

I held out my hands. "San Diego isn't Europe. It's only a couple of hours drive from LA."

Janie plucked a handful of chips out of the basket. She dropped them on the table and viciously pulverized them with the heel of her hand. "Given Sharon's precarious financial situation, the ex might as well be moving her children to Mars."

I said, "This doesn't seem right. I'd hire a lawyer and fight it."

Janie nodded. "I said the same thing. She can't afford a lawyer. And if she could, the ex has full custody. Given her history, the family court is unlikely to revise the custody to joint or the visitation rights order to an unsupervised status."

I shook my head. "Things changed in her favor. She's been working for a couple of months now. She's been at Winners Circle Swimwear and has written some business. They won't be shipping her orders until the end of March, so she hasn't earned any commissions yet. Maybe if she asked Allen Brown, her boss, he'd advance her a portion of her commissions?"

Janie's eyes flooded. "Sharon gave Allen my contact information in case of an emergency. He called two days ago and asked if I'd seen her lately?"

Huh? "Maybe she went out of town for business and had no time to check in with him. This has happened to me a few times."

Jane shook her head. "No. She made an appointment in the showroom and never showed up at the mart for it. Allen covered for her and made up an excuse as to why Sharon didn't make it to the meeting."

That got my attention. Buyers have a reputation of no respect for anyone's time but their own, so it is not unusual for one to stiff a vendor. But a seller ditching a buyer's appointment? Only if they want to lose the account.

"How weird. She doesn't have an industry reputation as undependable. But if she wants to keep the job, she better have a darned good excuse."

Janie shrugged. "No clue. I called Allen to ask, and he still hadn't heard from her. I told him she and I made plans to meet tonight and I said I'd ask where she's been. I called her a few times yesterday to discuss where to meet tonight, but I never reached her." She shredded her paper napkin into tiny pieces. "This isn't like her. I'm worried."

I looked at her oddly. "She lives above *your garage*. If she didn't return your calls, why didn't you go up to her place?"

Janie scrunched her nose. "I hated to come off as

either nosy or over-reacting if she had a perfectly good explanation."

She had to be joking.

I rolled my eyes. "Like what? If *she's sick*? Good golly, Miss Molly! If she is, her landlady is a *nurse*! If she is under the weather, you'd be her first call. You kept a key to her place, right?"

Janie nodded.

I grabbed the check, tossed two twenties on the table, and slid out of the booth. "Come on, Clara Barton." I pointed to the front door. "Get the lead out and let's go check on your tenant."

Chapter Twenty-Five

Twenty minutes later, Janie and I climbed up the narrow steps on the side of her garage and stood in front of Sharon's door. Although Janie held the key to the studio apartment, she knocked on the door first.

"Sha-ron," Janie called out in a sing-song voice. "It's me-Ja-ne. Are you okay, sweetie?"

Nothing.

Jane rapped on the door again. "Sharon, are you home?"

Still crickets.

I nudged Jane out of the way. "You need to put *a lot more* elbow grease into the knock and raise your voice above a conversation level if you want her to hear you."

Jane rolled her eyes and smirked, "Hol, this is a *studio apartment*. We're talking *one room* barely over five hundred square feet. It's not as if she's in *another room* and can't hear me. She's not ignoring me. She's not home." Jane put the key back in her pocket and turned around to go down the stairs. "Come on, let's go."

Logic said Jane was right, yet my gut said not so fast. "Janer, as long as we're here, let's take a look around. Even if she's not home, maybe we can still find something inside—a map, a scrap of paper with an address—some clue that might tell us where she went."

Jane nodded and took out the key. "Okay, but for giggles and squeaks, rap on the door again before we go barging in."

I yelled Sharon's name loud enough to wake up the dead and banged my fist against the door forcefully enough to loosen the hinges. Still, nothing doing. I twisted the door handle and gave it a slight push for the heck of it. The door creaked partially open. Our jaws dropped. *Who leaves their door unlocked in LA?* West Hollywood might not be the hood, yet no one confused it with Beverly Hills either.

I elbowed the door three-quarters of the way open. I sniffed and wrinkled my nose as we stepped into the tiny entry. The small space—a single eighteen by thirty room—smelled musty, as though unoccupied for a while. I did a visual one-eighty. It took only four Mississippis to eyeball the entire studio apartment.

The first thing I noticed? Not an inch of free space on any of the walls. All of them were covered with photographs of Sharon's two children.

In the back right corner, separated by a half-drawn open accordion curtain is a sink, toilet, and a coffin-like-stall shower that made the one on my houseboat seem luxuriously spacious by comparison. Other than discovering Sharon preferred a loofah to a washcloth and used an anti-dandruff shampoo, nothing of importance jumped out at us from a cursory inspection of the bathroom.

The bed was a twin-size Murphy style that you folded up and it disappeared into a closet. There were two other shallow closets divided by a stack of five shelves for groceries and clothes and no dresser.

A four-foot-wide kitchen in the back left corner. Two-burner cooktop, under-counter bar-sized refrigerator. A built-in microwave above a sink, and two storage cabinets.

A two-seater red Formica fifties-style dinette set separated the kitchen from the living room. The tufted red leatherette seat sporting hairpin legs facing the door? It was currently occupied by Sharon Hancock. Her stiff corpse was slumped over the table. Sharon's skin was red and swollen.

Naturally, I burst out laughing.

I held her back when Janie's training took over as she rushed to examine the body.

"Hol," Janie wriggled like a worm on a hook trying to extricate herself from my fingers clamped tight as a vise around her bicep. "Lemme go, for crying out loud! Maybe I can revive her."

I looked into Sharon's wide open sightless eyes staring out into space. I leaned over and gagged at the side of Sharon's bloated face lying in a dried pool of vomit laced with blood. I'm no doctor, but she sure looked deader than dead. While she didn't so much as twitch, I still passed my hand over her mouth to see if she was breathing. Not a puff of air either in or out grazed my fingers.

My cousin's eyes filled when I said, "Janer, trust me—there's *nothing* you can do for her. *She's gone.*"

Jane's shoulders slumped. She sighed, "You're right."

Sharon's bluish fingers were curled around the handle of a ceramic mug filled halfway with stale coffee. "*World's Best Mommy*" was painted in a child-like cursive scrawl across the mug's center. The crook of her left arm partially covered a typed note on the tabletop. I bent from the waist and turned my torso to be perpendicular and eye-level to the table. I angled my head to the right and faced the sheet of paper under Sharon's arm. I read the note out loud and my heart ached for Janie. "*I killed Leni Waxman. I can't live with the guilt. God forgive me.*"

Janie's voice cracked as she photographed the suicide note. "Wherever she is now, I pray she is at peace."

She took her cell phone out of her purse. "I'll call it in."

I held up my index finger. "Hold off for five minutes and let's take a quick look around."

Janie emphatically jerked her head from side to side. "*No way, Jose.* We have to report this *ASAP.*"

I rolled my eyes. "What's the big rush? A delay isn't the difference between *life and death.* Sharon is gonna be just as dead five minutes later as she is now."

Jane pursed her lips. "This is against my better judgment, but okay…five minutes, not a minute longer." Jane arched her eyebrows "I'm curious. *Why are we doing this?*"

Jane's lips formed a perfect O when I said, "Something tells me Sharon got some help getting dead." I opened the hobo and pulled an eyelash curler from my cosmetic kit.

Jane deadpanned. "While it's true you should be prepared if a cute cop answers the call, still it's kind of an odd time to do a touch-up."

A vision of Miguel's angry eyes flashed in my head. I held out a hand and sighed. "I'll pass. I have my hands full with the one cop I already dated." I waved the eyelash curler in the air. "It's not for a touch-up. I'll use these as tweezers. We don't want our fingerprints to screw up the scene. The cops get cranky if we touch anything or move stuff around. It fouls up the chain of evidence or something." I opened the photo app on my cell and handed the phone to Jane. "If we divide the room up into quadrants and work as a team, the search will go faster."

"What are we looking for?"

I shrugged. "No idea. We'll recognize it when we see it. Anything odd or out of place."

What could be odder or more out of place than a stiff slumped over a dinette table? I kept that unsettling thought to myself.

The focal point of the room—Matching beige corduroy loveseat and easy chair. Both had seen better days. Small portable TV. Particle board coffee table. A lidless mayonnaise jar serving as a vase containing a bouquet of gorgeous blood-red roses sat on top of a faded dishtowel in the upper corner of the coffee table.

We sat side by side on the loveseat to examine the sheaf of documents the Waxmans gave to Sharon that lay fanned out on the coffee table. I opened and closed the eyelash curler like the maw of a hungry shark. "I'll turn the pages of the documents after you photograph each one."

Jane pointed to presumably Sharon's handwriting on the second page. "Look at the notes Sharon made in the margins. She wrote questions and counteroffer proposals. She didn't end up accepting it, but at least at some point, Sharon considered accepting their offer."

I pursed my lips. "Maybe, maybe not. These notes? Could be only for show. No love was lost between Sharon and the Waxman women. Sharon's words: '*A Waxman is a Waxman. And trust me, the apple didn't fall far from the tree.*' Sharon didn't negotiate with Hadassah and her brother in good faith. She never revealed she'd been working for Allen before the Hanukkah party."

Janie sighed when I said, "The truth is she betrayed their trust and double-crossed them by weaponizing the documents against them. Sharon tried her best to get Rapido kicked off the Allied Stores vendor matrix."

As I shuffled the pages of the Waxman documents back into order another sheet of paper fluttered to the floor. I gingerly picked it up with the eyelash curler and laid it face-up on the coffee table. My eyes bugged as I read the heading: *Ginsburg & Goldstein, Esquires, Attorneys-at-Law.* Janie squealed with delight while I read the letter out loud.

Dear Ms. Hancock:

We are honored you considered our firm for your legal representation. As a Family Law practice, our goal at G & G is to diligently fight for our clients and get justice for every one of them, regardless of their financial situation. During our twenty years in business, we've been fortunate to build an extremely successful practice. Success comes with a moral responsibility to pay it back by paying it forward. To accomplish this goal, we created a Special Needs Account for us to draw upon when exceptional cases like yours require a pro bono financial arrangement.

As such, we have accepted you as a client at no cost to you. Please come in and sign the client agreement at your earliest convenience so we can present a strategy and upon your approval, proceed to file a cease-and-desist order in Family Court to temporarily prevent your ex-husband from moving your children out of Los Angeles County.

We look forward to working closely with you. We

promise to work vigorously to achieve the best possible outcome for you and your children.
    Sincerely Yours,
    Leah Ginsburg, Managing Partner,
    Ginsburg & Goldstein, Esq. Attorneys-at-Law

I said, "Could be Sharon has been unavailable because she's been working with her lawyers."

Janie sucked in her cheeks. "I hope that is the reason…Considering how upset she got over the kids moving to San Diego, it's awfully strange she didn't share the good news."

I said, "Maybe she wanted to wait until she had something more concrete to report."

We finished photographing the documents and moved on to the kitchen, where a coffee-stained empty cup and chipped saucer sat in the porcelain sink.

I pointed to the two items in the sink. "Sharon had company recently."

Janie photographed the two items in the sink from all angles. "Not necessarily. Maybe those are from breakfast and she didn't get around to washing them."

I shook my head. "Makes no sense. Why would she dirty an extra cup and saucer when she already had her mug filled with coffee? Nope. Someone else drank from that cup."

Janie shrugged. "If she entertained company, it's impossible to determine if Sharon died before or after the visitor left. Rigor has set in, so she has been dead for at least four hours."

Janie bent over Sharon's battered corpse and sighed. "From the condition of her body, one thing is for sure. Sharon didn't die of natural causes."

Nothing gets past you, Florence Nightingale.

I glanced at the documents on the coffee table. I might stink at math, but one and one don't add up to three. Why would Sharon kill herself if there was a chance to get her children back? It makes no sense. Or did she commit suicide? Up until an hour ago, Sharon was my number one suspect. My gut still says she is, yet my heart says not so fast.

Until this mystery was figured out, there was only one thing to do.

Detective Jones answered on the second ring. "Hello, Detective Jones. Holly Schlivnik here. Good news, Detective. You can close the book on Leni Waxman's murder. I'm standing next to Leni's killer, and she confessed."

Chapter Twenty-Six

After I finished relating the weekend festivities to the Yentas Monday morning, Joan stared me down over the rims of her eyeglasses as only she does.

"*You really told Detective Jones you stood next to Leni's killer and she confessed*?"

I batted my eyes. "I don't see the problem. My information was accurate. I *was* standing right next to Sharon when I called Detective Jones. And Sharon *did confess*."

Joan cocked a brow. "It never *occurred to you* to tell the detective the killer was *dead*?"

I shrugged. "He would find out soon enough. Why spoil the surprise?"

Sonia stifled a grin. "So, an army of cops stormed the place?"

I burst out laughing. "Oh, yeah. The scene? Right out of central casting for your garden-variety TV police drama. Jones led the parade followed by six heavily-armed uniforms behind him. My cousin Janie almost wet her panties when Jones yelled, 'Drop your weapons.' If your life depended on it, you couldn't find a square inch of the room not filled with wall-to-wall cops all trying to clear a studio apartment."

Hope clucked her tongue. "I bet Jones was mad as a wet hen. You're lucky he didn't shoot you on general principles."

Hope was right. Of course, after Jones delivers his report to his superior, my erstwhile favorite police captain might consider it. I rolled my eyes. "Cops need a sense of humor."

Queenie asked, "What about Gary's release?"

I funneled my lips. "I called Ms. M. and filled her in as soon as Detective Jones allowed us to leave. I spoke to her again last night. After almost two days, she and Jones are still going round and round over Gary's release. Jones won't authorize it until the results of Sharon's autopsy and the forensic tests being run on the suicide note are in." I spat. "According to Snip, it could take at least a week."

Queenie blew the air out of her cheeks. "I'm not surprised. He pulled the same runaround crap on Ms. M. before authorizing my release."

****

I went through the motions at work the rest of the day, but visions of Sharon's corpse and Gary languishing in jail making a continuous loop around in my brain made focusing on anything else impossible. After a restless night of tossing and turning, I was still in a fog when I got to work on Tuesday. Late afternoon I called Ms. M. Regrettably, she was no closer to getting Gary sprung from the hoosegow than the last time I'd checked.

Try as I might to accomplish anything all afternoon, I got nothing done at the office. His intransigence so disgusted me that I could have throttled Detective Jones. I had to do *something productive to stay busy* or left to my own devices, I'd come up with something stupid enough to land me in the cell next to Gary. I printed up all the photos Jane took on my phone and headed home. Maybe I'd find something somewhere in all those photos to convince the myopically stubborn cop that Sharon murdered Leni.

I went through the docs with a fine-tooth comb. Something wasn't Kosher, but after three thorough passes through them, whatever it was still eluded me. Then it hit me. The *wording* wasn't the problem. It's the *type* on the Rapido docs. Several letters—I, L, and G— are deformed. Hmm. Documents—typed on a typewriter, not on a computer. Three of the keys were broken. If typed on a computer, the letters would not be deformed. It's odd for a big company like Rapido or Barry Waxman's law firm not to draw these documents up on a computer.

Mental head slap. My line of reasoning might not be necessarily correct. The issue could be in the computer's programming. Or was the printer the problem? If the printer copied it blurry it could appear as a damaged typewriter key. I closed my eyes to picture the studio apartment. Something was missing. Bingo. Bongo. Jackpot. We'd gone through every possible place to store one, and there wasn't a typewriter or a computer anywhere in the room. Maybe Sharon owned a laptop. We didn't see one in the apartment. It's possible she left it in her car. If she typed the note on a computer, we didn't see a printer in Sharon's place. Perhaps she used one of those twenty-four-hour copier services nearby. Or maybe she typed and printed the note at Allen's factory.

Or. Maybe. Possible. Perhaps. Good grief. I rubbed my eyes and checked the time. Eleven O'clock on the dot. Crap, I'd been at this for almost four hours and so far for all my trouble, the only thing I gained is a clearer understanding of the way Siggie feels when he chases his tail. I took a restorative glug of coffee and my innards twisted around like a pretzel. The answers to my questions *must be here* in these photos *somewhere.* Considering my piss-poor investigative skills, they were probably staring me in the face.

Wait a Cincinnati minute. My sleuthing prowess might not be as lame as it appeared. I reread the suicide note and it came to me in a flash. Sure enough. My eyes bugged as I compared the print on the suicide note to the documents the Waxmans gave Sharon. *The three deformed letters on the documents from them are the same ones on Sharon's suicide note.* The typewriter must be at Rapido headquarters. How about Barry's law firm? Nah, law firms as big as his are strictly computerized, so I tossed the theory out of my head as fast as it came to mind. Besides, if they used typewriters, it would be difficult for Sharon to gain access. Either Sharon met the Waxmans at the Rapido building and typed the suicide note there—or I stumbled across evidence that a Waxman murdered Sharon Hancock and made it look like a suicide. Holy guacamole.

This couldn't wait until morning. I reached for the phone to call Snip. Doubt kept my fingers from pushing her speed dial number. I might be wrong about this. It's happened before. Who am I kidding? I'm wrong most of the time. So, waking my early-rising friend on a fool's errand wasn't a brain surgeon move. Instead, I spent a sleepless night pacing the length of the houseboat unsuccessfully trying to make sense of it all.

Chapter Twenty-Seven

Bleary-eyed, at the crack of dawn, I gathered all the docs and photos spread out across the galley table and shoved them into my messenger bag.

Snip always got to work early. I called her to ask about Sharon's autopsy. She said she hadn't started it yet because there were six patients ahead of Sharon. She promised to move Heaven and Earth to perform the autopsy and push the lab for a rush on the test results in forty-eight hours. We optimistically made dinner plans for Thursday night.

Despite an invigorating hot shower, a change of clothes, and a mug of coffee strong enough to take the first layer of paint off the convertible, I still looked like overcooked crap. Yet I was remarkably functional.

I dropped Siggie off at doggie daycare and headed downtown. Gunmetal-gray storm clouds darkened the marina and only became more ominous as I drove east on Interstate 10. Crap on a crumpet. No doubt the forecast included a soaking. By the time I arrived at the mart, it started to drizzle. Rain at rush hour in this burg? The commute home is sure to be a real kick in the pants.

I never held anything back from the Yentas before—especially from Queenie. I made an executive decision to delay sharing anything until after I met with Snip. I crossed my fingers behind my back while I blamed the raccoon rings of fatigue under my puffy eyes on a noisy fight between two alley cats that kept me and all my dock neighbors up all night.

I'd no sooner settled into my chair in the showroom when my cell phone rang. The caller ID said, Johnny. Hot diggity dog.

"Hey, Johnny. If the convertible is almost ready, what time can I pick her up? If it's before the end of the day, I might need to move some things around."

"Sorry to disappoint you, Holly Swimsuit. The police towed your car back to my garage only an hour ago. I've ordered the part, but it hasn't come in yet. I put in a call to the supplier to goose the delivery. Regrettably, they don't stock every part for a classic car like yours. They're doing their best to get it from the manufacturer. The reality? Don't expect your car back for another week."

"*You just got the car back*? Good gravy, what did the cops find that took so long?"

"No clue. I asked. Since I'm only the mechanic and not the car owner, forget about them sharing any information. The paperwork inside the car said you'll get their report in the mail."

It rained continuously all day. I got to the mart parking structure late afternoon and discovered the flat tire. This is LA. Unless an El Nino hits, it doesn't rain much here, so no one knows the right way to drive in it. However, when it rains, it rains cats and dogs, day and night. We're not talking about a leaky faucet. Think grab all the animals and build the Ark kind of rain. The Santa Monica freeway probably resembled a demolition derby track by now.

If I called the auto club and luck broke my way, maybe they'd get a tow truck to the mart by next

Tuesday. For giggles and squeaks, I called anyway on the off-chance I underestimated their inclement weather preparedness. As if. I listened to a recording thanking me for my many years as a loyal customer and asking me to please accept their apologies for any inconvenience they created, however, they were too busy to solve my problem for the foreseeable future. To add insult to injury, the recording disconnected me. Twice.

Fortunately, my dad insisted his kids learn to change a tire. I opened the trunk, and hauled the spare out, along with the jack and a heavy lug wrench. Before I positioned the jack under the jack point, I rolled up my sleeves and cringed. I wore an expensive lavender silk blouse and a new pair of gray gabardine pants for the first time. Spiffy ensemble, just not the best outfit to play grease monkey.

I am an independent woman, but my mother didn't raise stupid children. I needed a knight in shining armor. I checked around the parking garage. I waited for ten minutes. Regrettably, no hero appeared. No doubt he could be found upstairs at The Showroom bar for happy hour getting sloshed with all the other heroes waiting out the storm. Sitting around all night waiting for help to arrive wasn't an option. I gritted my teeth and reasoned in addition to my mechanic, the guy who ran the dry cleaners also had kids I'd be helping to put through college.

I jacked the car, got the lug nuts off, switched out the flat for the spare, and managed not to ruin my trousers. I ran my fingers over the flat. There is always a lot of construction around the mart. Did I run over a nail? Sure enough, a big fat one was embedded deep in the tread. I shoved the flat and the changing kit in the trunk and drove to the gas station. Johnny swapped my flat for another spare and I headed to the marina, picked up my pup and a takeaway pizza, and enjoyed relaxing a few hours thanks to a gigantic glass of Chardonnay.

The next evening, the rental car listed to the left so badly, that the flat was visible from the mart parking structure elevator bank. The auto club guy changed the flat and put on the tire Johnny patched the day before. The first one, okay an inconvenience, more complicated by the rain, no biggie; everyone gets a flat tire. But two days in a row? Cripes, give me a break.

Chapter Twenty-Eight

Thursday night I met Snip at Pasta at the Pier, a cozy locals-favorite on the Washington Street Pier featuring panoramic windows for a gorgeous ocean view and serving the best antipasto this side of Florence, Italy.

While I almost split my spleen in anticipation of getting the lowdown on Sharon's autopsy, I'd never rush into questions before my favorite coroner's voracious appetite is sated. First Snip polished off most of our antipasto appetizer and a second glass of Chianti. Next, she devoured her usual half-pasta/half-pizza pie combo entrée and longingly eyed my lobster ravioli. *Finally*, after she consumed the only garlic breadstick left in the basket—the last item of uneaten food on the table—I made my move.

"Have you completed Sharon Hancock's autopsy?"

Snip nodded.

"You called the COD?"

"Yes. The victim died from cardiovascular collapse and hypovolemic shock due to acute arsenic poisoning."

I batted my eyes. "For those of us who missed this particular lecture in med school, Hypovolemic shock is…"

"Hypovolemic shock is an emergency condition in which severe blood or other fluid loss makes the heart unable to pump enough blood to the body. This type of shock causes many organs to shut down and stop working."

I widened my eyes. "You said *Arsenic*? As in Arsenic and Old Lace?"

Snip smiled. "As in an arsenic-based herbicide."

"What's an herbicide?"

Snip donned her professor's cap. "In laymen's terms? Weed killer. There are many options readily available in the gardening section of a big box or home improvement store. Arsenic-based herbicides include MSMA-short for monosodium methanearsonate as well DSMA-short for disodium methanearsonate. Add arsenic trioxide; sodium arsenite; and arsenates of sodium, potassium, calcium, and lead as well as Bipyridyl-dipyridyl herbicides to the list. The fatal human dose for ingested arsenic trioxide is 70 to 180 milligrams (mg) or around 600 micrograms per kilograms (kg)/day."

Snip pursed her lips. "Eighty-five milligrams of Paraquat in the victim's system as well as 20 milligrams of the same herbicide in the coffee cup next to the victim's hand. Miss Hancock ingested enough *Paraquat* to fell an elephant."

"What is that stuff?"

"Paraquat is a toxic chemical widely used as an herbicide-primarily for weed and grass control. In the United States, paraquat is available primarily as a liquid in various strengths. After a person ingests a large amount of Paraquat, he or she is immediately going to be in pain and experience swelling of the mouth and throat. The next signs of illness following ingestion are gastrointestinal-digestive tract symptoms, such as nausea, vomiting, which might become bloody, abdominal pain, and diarrhea, which may also become bloody. The symptoms the victim exhibited—red, swollen skin, bloody vomit, bluish fingers—pointed us in the direction of some type of poisoning. The tox test sealed the Paraquat deal."

I grimaced. "Good gravy, what a horrible way to kill yourself." I tapped my lower lip. "She sure picked a gruesome way to do it. I'd overdose on sleeping pills. You swallow a bottleful of pills, go to sleep, and don't wake up."

Snip dipped her head. "Maybe it was a spur-of-the-moment decision and she didn't keep sleeping pills in the house."

I smirked. "So, instead of going to a pharmacy and buying over-the-counter sleeping pills, she hit her neighborhood big box store and bought *weed killer*?"

Snip laughed. "Not likely. If she hadn't pre-planned to kill herself and had no sleeping pills handy, she might have lost her nerve to follow through with the suicide by the time she went to a drugstore. She lived in a studio apartment over a garage. The house featured both a front and backyard lawn. Maybe she went into the garage and found the weed killer and used it simply because it *was available*."

In *my cousin's* garage? Get real.

"Sharon's landlady is my *cousin Janie*. We come from a family of black thumbs capable of killing cacti. Trust me, Janie's no Luther Burbank. Janie is a *nurse*, not a gardener. She isn't one to mow the lawn, prune the hedges, or *kill any weeds*. Ask Detective Jones to get Jane's permission to search her garage. I guarantee he won't find *any* gardening apparatus, let alone weed killer. Jane's lawns are pristine only because she isn't the one taking care of them. Believe me, Janie hired a *gardener.*"

Snip funneled her lips. "It begs the question: how did the arsenic get in the victim's coffee cup?"

I arched a brow. "Better yet—*who* put the arsenic in Sharon's coffee cup? Did the lab run the fingerprints on the suicide note and Sharon's mug as well as the cup and saucer in the kitchen?"

"The victim's fingerprints are the only ones on the mug in her hand."

"And the suicide note and the cup and saucer in the kitchen sink?"

Snip scratched the crown of her hair. "Inconclusive."

My eyes bugged. "*Inconclusive*? How is that possible?"

Snip snapped her fingers. "Simple. The fingerprints on those items were not a match to the victim's nor any in the statewide database."

I fanned out my fingers on the tabletop. "Well, they might not belong to Sharon, but *somebody's* fingerprints are on them."

Snip held out her hands and wiggled her digits in the air. "Maybe the victim wore gloves?"

I pointed to Snip's empty wine glass. "And maybe you ought to lay off the sauce. *Are you nuts*?" I huffed, "Janie and I went through every nook and cranny of the studio. There were no gloves anywhere in the apartment."

Snip blushed red as a ripe tomato from her neck to her hairline. "Okay, you're right." She waved her dismissal of the ridiculous notion as though swatting a pesky fly at a picnic.

Ya think, Doctor Death?

I sighed. "I *wanted* Sharon to be Leni's killer and to have *committed suicide* when she became overcome by guilt. Regarding the suicide? My gut says otherwise. While Sharon Hancock suffered from her share of problems—some of them serious and difficult to overcome—she never struck me as one to throw in the towel and do herself in. She had too much to live for." I ticked off my reasons on my fingers. "According to Jane, Sharon was as devoted a mother as possible, given her circumstances. She would *never* leave her children, especially by killing herself. Sharon was hysterical over the ex-husband moving the kids to San Diego. Despite the odds against her, she was determined to fight it. And she did. Ginsburg & Goldstein is LA's premier Family Law Firm and they agreed to take her case pro bono. Remember the world's best mommy mug in her hand and all the walls in the house were covered by pictures of her children? She started a new job and was optimistic about the chance to revive her career." I looked Snip in the eye. "This is not the way a woman contemplating suicide behaves."

Snip asked, "So, are you saying Ms. Hancock *didn't murder* Ms. Waxman? Then as much as you may hate to accept it…Gary Burkett is likely the murderer."

I slapped my palm on the table hard enough to spill half of my Chianti. "*No*! I'm not saying that at all. I'm positive Sharon murdered Leni. But I doubt she killed herself."

Snip rolled her eyes and handed me her napkin. "Then who killed Ms. Hancock?"

I dabbed our two napkins over the tabletop to mop up the spilled Chianti. "My vote goes to the person whose fingerprints are on the suicide note and the cup and saucer in the sink."

"Any idea how to prove it?"

I waved my digits. "Compare the fingerprints on those items to the ones on the documents on Sharon's coffee table. You'll find the print on the documents and the suicide note all typed by the same three deformed letters, so they were probably typed on the same machine. The machine is either located in the Rapido executive office or Barry Waxman's law firm. Ask Detective Jones to get a judge to issue a subpoena for Hadassah and Barry Waxman's fingerprints."

My friend sighed with the depth of sadness of someone who always delivered bad news. "You may have unmasked Ms. Hancock's killers. You probably sealed Mr. Burkett's fate as well."

Chapter Twenty-Nine

Janie and I attended Sharon's funeral on Monday morning, so I missed the Yenta coffee klatch. Bright and early Tuesday, I served the coffee and brought the girls up to speed.

"Sharon's funeral was held in the garden Chapel on the grounds of The San Fernando Mission. Janie and I waited our turn in the vestibule to sign the guest book and pick up a prayer book before going inside for the service. We moved a up few spaces when a bony finger poked me between the shoulder blades. It turned out to be Snip, who came to the service with Dr. Sherry Silverman. Sherry is a med school friend of Snip's whom I met last summer. She is a Psychiatrist affiliated with the same hospital where my cousin works as an emergency room nurse. *Sharon* was one of Sherry's patients."

I glanced around the table and soldiered on. "We got to the head of the line, signed the guest book, picked up a prayer book, and the four of us proceeded into the chapel. As I turned to take my seat, I nodded hello to *Detective Jones* who stood in a corner observing who entered the chapel."

Hope asked, "Why did a *homicide detective* go to the funeral? The word is Sharon committed suicide."

I said, "I met Snip for dinner and she revealed Sharon died of a massive dose of *a weed killer* called

Paraquat. The lab found enough of this stuff in Sharon's system and in her coffee mug to take down an elephant."

Sonia grimaced. "An awful way to die."

Joan nodded. "I'm no suicide expert, however, much less invasive ways exist to end it all."

Queenie tapped her index finger on the tip of her nose. "No kidding. I'd opt for an OD of sleeping pills."

I snapped my fingers. "I said the same thing to Snip. No containers of weed killer were found in Sharon's apartment or Janie's garage—or sleeping pills either." I held out my hands. "And *no one* makes a trip to a store expressly to buy *weed killer* as a means to commit suicide. However, it's a Jim Dandy way to *murder* somebody. Paraquat is easy to mix with food, water, or other beverages. If the form of paraquat used does not contain the safeguard additives—dye, odor, and vomiting agent, people might not be aware the food, water, or other beverages are contaminated. Eating or drinking paraquat-contaminated food or beverages, especially in large quantities would fatally poison unwitting victims."

Sonia said, "So, Sharon's death has now been declared a murder and not a suicide?"

I said, "According to Snip, after the information I gave her, Detective Jones is leaning in that direction. Remember I told you that after my cousin Jane and I discovered Sharon dead, a few things raised some questions, so we took photographs of everything that struck us as odd?"

I grinned. "You girls know how antsy I get if one and one doesn't add up to two. I printed up all the photos and took them home. Something about one set of photos seemed odd, but the issue didn't come to me until I compared the print on the documents the Waxmans gave Sharon to the print on the suicide note under Sharon's arm. All were typed with the same three deformed letters, so they were most likely typed on the same machine. We didn't find a printer or copier in Sharon's house, so the machine that printed both the documents and the suicide letter was either located in the Rapido executive office or Barry Waxman's law firm. I told Snip to ask Detective Jones to get a judge to issue a subpoena for Hadassah and Barry Waxman's fingerprints…and surprise, surprise…the Waxmans are fighting the subpoena."

Sonia asked, "Was the Chapel full?"

I made a quick mental head count. "The Chapel holds around one hundred and sixty guests. I eyeballed the crowd at somewhere between twenty-five and thirty percent of the Chapel's capacity."

Hope's eyes filled. "It's sad so few people cared enough about Sharon to pay their last respects."

Joan asked, "What about Sharon's family?"

I shrugged. "Not many came to the funeral. Five of them sat in the front row on the left side of the Chapel."

Joan asked, "Were Sharon's children at the funeral?" Joan shuddered. "I'd never subject children *so young* to a funeral mass."

I said, "They were both there. Sharon's ex and her two children entered the Chapel last before the pallbearers escorted the casket to the altar. The ex-husband took the kids over to Sharon's family to say hello, but they didn't sit next to them. And Janie didn't want to make a scene, so she didn't go up to the kids and their father to pay her respects when they greeted Sharon's family."

Sonia held out her hands. "They didn't sit in the family section?"

"Nope."

Hope looked at me strangely. "Did they sit by themselves?"

"Nope."

The Yentas' jaws dropped when I said, "You'll *never guess* who they sat next to. I almost fell off my seat when Sharon's ex and the kids went to the front row of the Chapel and sat next to *Hadassah and Barry Waxman*!"

Joan tapped her cheeks. "No kidding? I'm surprised they knew one another."

I said, "Me too and it gets better. After the merger of their two firms, Barry Waxman and Sharon's ex-husband are now law partners."

Queenie funneled her lips. "So, the Waxmans killed Sharon? Their motive is…?"

I said, "The documents in Sharon's house were an employment agreement the Waxmans offered to Sharon. She strung them along and had no intention of signing the agreement since she'd been working for Allen Brown before the Hanukkah party. Sharon double-crossed the Waxmans and tried her best to get Rapido thrown out of the Allied competitive swimwear program. I met Hadassah for coffee and told her about Sharon and Allen's meeting with Sue Ellen. I can't prove Hadassah acted on the information and went after Sharon. Needless to say, Hadassah was not a happy camper."

Joan tapped a spoon on her coffee cup. "If the Waxmans are fighting a subpoena for their fingerprints, they have something to hide."

Sonia stroked her chin. "And the plot thickens."

Joan narrowed her eyes. "So, let's say for the sake of argument, either a Waxman or Sharon's ex murdered Sharon. If so, do we eliminate her as Leni Waxman's killer?"

Queenie said, "If so…and Gary is innocent, we're right back where we started. Who killed Leni?"

I turned up my nose. "My money is still on Sharon. Now that she's dead it's going to be harder to prove it—especially if it turns out she didn't write the suicide note or do herself in."

Hope circled back to the funeral. "I've never attended a Catholic memorial service, what was the funeral like?"

I swiped a wrist across my forehead. "*A lot* shorter than I expected. From the time the pallbearers brought the coffin up to the altar and the priest blessed the coffin with Holy Water, said the Lord's Prayer, led the attendees in a hymn, and gave a short eulogy, the service ended in thirty minutes."

I took a sip of coffee and continued. "We made a group decision to skip the internment and refreshments at the Mission social hall after the burial. We were famished and anxious to unwind from a taxing morning, so we ended up at Los Gauchos, the oldest Mexican restaurant in San Fernando. While scarfing down chips and margaritas, Snip said Sherry dragged her to the wake Sharon's uncle hosted for his niece at the social hall of his Parish in Pasadena."

I glanced around the table. "The uncle and Sharon's ex-husband are old poker partners and still friendly, and the ex was invited to the wake. Like most wakes, there was plenty of booze to go around and the ex-husband had too much to drink. Sherry noticed the ex-husband weaving over the open casket and talking to the corpse. It turns out Sherry was a practical joker who loved to throw her voice. Sherry decided to pay the ex-husband back for all the rotten things he pulled on Sharon. The shrink stood behind the ex and threw her voice. She said, *'I never really loved you. And by the way, you were lousy in bed.'*

I slapped my palm on the table and laughed. "The ex-husband fainted."

Chapter Thirty

The next day nothing went right—first sales reps crabbed about late deliveries and then cranky buyers complained they couldn't sell empty hangers—another problem was *the last thing* I needed. Unfortunately, when I reached the rental car, the good news was another flat tire. If you have those odds, you better go to Vegas and bet the farm. My luck, I got the same auto club guy from the previous time. When he suggested I'd save a lot of money and aggravation if I ditched the car concept and considered public transportation, I gave the smartass the mental middle finger salute. Everyone in LA is a wannabe comedian.

I drove back to Johnny's station and left the rental. Three flats in less than a week? Get real. I wanted answers. Queenie met me at the station, shuttled me home, and the next morning she gave me a lift to the mart. Before I sat at my desk, the phone rang: caller ID said Johnny. One flat tire, two tires with damaged treads, and three valves were damaged. The verdict? All four tires needed to be replaced. Cripes, I couldn't catch a break. In addition to the exorbitant rental fee, I'd be shelling out a small fortune to repair a car that isn't mine. Not even halfway over, and already the week turned into a doozy. I shuddered, imagining what the next calamity would be. Regrettably, I didn't have long to find out...

Johnny and I ended our conversation and I noticed a

plain white envelope with my name typed on the front sitting on my blotter. I waved it at Patti, our showroom manager. "Who left this?"

She shrugged, "No idea. I found it on the floor when I opened up this morning."

I slit open the envelope and unfolded a single sheet of paper. My blood ran cold as I read the first line.

"Holy crap," I choked. "Queenie, come over here."

Queenie's voice quavered with alarm. "W-what's the m-matter? You're w-white as a g-ghost." She read the note and took a step back as though fending off a blow. "*Oh. My. Goddess.*"

Someone cut out the letters from magazines so the note spelled out:

DoN'T STicK yOuR NosE WherE It DOesN'T BeLOng

Or yOU wIlL ENd Up ThE SamE wAy aS The OtHeRs

mIND yOUr OwN BUsinEsS YoU HavE BEeN wARnEd

I make my share of bonehead decisions, but I am smart enough to recognize if the time has come to involve someone who carries a gun and wears a badge. I grabbed my purse, borrowed Queenie's car keys, and announced I'd be back after getting answers.

An hour later I left the Rampart division station furious enough to pitch forty fits. Detective Jones's reaction to the threatening note? To chastise me for interfering again in his case. I stormed out of Jones's office and stomped down the hall to Miguel's. After all, why date a police captain if you can't pull rank once in a while? Big mistake. After enduring a blistering lecture from the good captain on the merits of minding my own business and possibly staying alive, I left the cop shop dragging my tail between my legs. After a long day at work, I spent another restless night pacing the houseboat questioning everything. As I paced, I read and reread the threatening note and grew angrier each time. Nobody threatens Holly Schlivnik and gets off Scot free. If the cops wouldn't help, I'll figure it out on my own. They say the Goddess helps those who help themselves. I sure hoped this was one of those times.

****

My mood didn't improve the next morning when Johnny handed me the eye-popping bill for the new tires and informed me the convertible would not be ready until the middle of the following week.

How does a girl chase away the blues? Shopping, of course! And I had the perfect companion. My shopaholic friend Christine and I were long overdue for a get-together. Chris lives in the valley and I am at the beach, so we take turns going to the other one's hood. It was my turn to go into the valley, so we made plans to meet at the swimwear department in Bainbridge Department Store in the Encino Hills Fashion Galleria at six.

With two Chatty Cathy dolls like us, our gabfest will no doubt last late into the night. I asked my neighbor Muriel to pick Siggie up from doggie daycare and keep him for the night. Muriel never said no—she loves my hound almost as much as I do.

If you live *anywhere* in the greater Los Angeles area, one guarantee you can count on is that traffic will be a constant part of your life. The 405 freeway and the canyons that bisect the Santa Monica mountains separating Los Angeles from the San Fernando Valley both run north-south and parallel to one another. While the distance from downtown to the 405 isn't far, at rush hour it takes quite a while to get from the clogged Interstate 10 west to the 405 north. By the time you get onto the 405, both directions are always a nightmare. By comparison, cutting diagonally across town to Hollywood and taking Coldwater Canyon Avenue into the valley is much faster. So, even considering canyon traffic, over the hill is the faster way to the valley from my part of downtown at that time of day.

At dusk, I turned onto Sunset from Fountain Avenue in the heart of Hollywood and merged onto Coldwater Canyon northbound. The unlit two-lane canyon road turned pitch black after the sun set twenty minutes later. Traffic was heavy until I got to the summit. As I descended, the city-side residential traffic thinned out substantially. The downgrade of the canyon road was gradual but the curves became sharper and steeper the farther north I drove. So, while fewer cars rode on the north side of the mountain road, I kept my speed under twenty miles per hour, including on the straightaways.

A car traveling way too fast for a two-lane mountain road pulled up behind me as I passed The Canyon Market parking lot. As we came out of a hairpin curve a quarter-mile later, the driver sped up and almost blinded me when he flashed his bright lights. I pulled as far to the right as I dared to give him enough room and signaled with my high beams for the idiot to pass me. Instead, he flashed his brights again and laid on the horn. What was this jerk's problem? He blasted the horn again and closed the distance between us. A string of cars traveled southbound, so he couldn't pass me, and I had no room anywhere else to go. My heart pounded hard as a jackhammer as I wiped a sheen of perspiration dotting my forehead off with the cuff of my shirt sleeve.

We rounded the next curve and I clutched the steering wheel in a white-knuckled death grip when he banged into my back fender. It was too dark to get a good look at the vehicle. From the size of the jolt, it had to be either an SUV or a pickup truck driven by a crazy person apparently in such a hurry, that he was willing to run my car off the road to pass me.

I misjudged the angle of the next turn and hit the brake too hard as the car careened around the curve. As we came into the center of curvature, the new tires I just paid a king's ransom for screamed their complaint when the maniac rammed the rental's bumper so forcefully that it skidded in a hard right toward the side of the sheer cliff.

I frantically wracked my brain to recall the high school driver's ed teacher's instruction on the method to steer safely when in a skid. Miraculously, I remembered his caution *not to react the logical way and steer in the opposition of the skid as this specific move is a sure way to flip the car and roll.* I kept my foot on the accelerator and steered in the direction of the skid, then I ran out of the road. The lunatic rammed me again for good measure. The rental shimmied and fishtailed off the pavement into a shallow layer of gravel then slammed into the runaway truck berm at the edge of the cliff.

The crazy guy lost control of his car and it clipped the end of the berm and spun around to the precipice. I stared gape-mouthed in horror as momentum took control and the huge SUV sailed over the edge of the cliff into oblivion.

Then the world went black.

Chapter Thirty-One

The incessant beeping roused me groggy and disoriented out of fitful sleep.

A familiar voice chirped a waaaay-too cheery greeting. "Good morning, sunshine. Welcome back."

Welcome back from...? I cracked open an eye and groaned. "Marvelous. If you're standing over me, I must be dead."

My favorite medical examiner chortled her reply. "Good to see you haven't lost your sense of humor yet."

Who's joking?

I surveyed my surroundings and realized the bed I occupied wasn't mine. "Where am I?"

She said, "Encino Oaks Community Hospital."

"How did you find out I was here?"

"Miguel was notified and called AJ and she called me. AJ's out in the field now on a case. She said to tell you she'll be here as soon as possible."

I shuddered as memories of the awful event of the day before came flooding back.

I yelped, "Oh my God, Siggie and my boat! I've gotta get out of here!" I raised my head to get out of bed and the searing pain behind my eyes brought a galaxy of stars.

Snip eased me back onto the mattress. "Relax! AJ contacted your dockmaster who reached your neighbor. Muriel packed Siggie up and turned him over to AJ. He's probably having a ball visiting Peso by now and your boat is fine. Try not to move around unnecessarily. The more you rest your body, the faster you will heal. You're down for the count. Lay still, if you want to recover before the next ice age."

No kidding. Every part of my body ached.

It took too much energy for me to keep up my end of the banter, so I closed my eyes.

Snip leaned over and tsk-tsked as she stuck an ice-cold stethoscope between my boobs. Satisfied my heart still beat, she put her index and middle finger on my swollen left wrist to check my pulse rate. Next, she shined a blinding beam from a penlight-sized flashlight in my eyes and I smacked her hand away.

She said, "Considering the whack against the car window your noggin took, it's amazing you didn't break the glass or crack open your head. All you got is a goose egg on the side of your head and a slight concussion." Snip lightly smacked the left side of her head to demonstrate. "It's a good thing you're such a hardhead."

I made a sour face and a kaleidoscope of light lit behind my eyes. I snapped. "I realize your other patients don't talk back, so you're obviously out of practice. No offense Doctor Death; your bedside manner stinks. Your delivery needs some fine-tuning."

She held out her hands. "Hey, I'm just sayin'."

Friends. Go figure. Geesh.

She glanced at a chart hanging on the bedframe and smiled. "You took a licking, and you're still ticking."

Nothing gets past you, Doctor Quincy.

Her concerned eyes searched mine. "How are you doing?"

I took a few beats to inventory my issues before I

replied. My ability to move was hampered by an aching, heavily bandaged left shoulder, left hip, and midsection. An IV was stuck in my right arm, and it hurt to move my left wrist. My arms, face, and chest were burnt and a foul-smelling ointment oozed over my skin. I wiggled my toes and an electric zap of pain raced the length of my spine. I tried taking a deep breath and almost fainted. I raised my head off the pillow and the stars exploded behind my eyes. I touched the goose egg-sized knot pulsating pain on the left side of my head.

I ran a finger over my lips swollen as fat as two inner tubes. I opened my achy jaw and it creaked like the scratch of a rusty gate. My sandpapery tongue seemed as thick as a brick and too big for my mouth. I couldn't raise my arm past my boobs to massage my temples to ease the jackhammer banging inside my head. Even my hair hurt. Otherwise, doing peachy. "It's a tossup of either the mother of all hangovers, or I've been run over by a train."

Snip laughed. "Close, but no cigar. Try not to move around unnecessarily. The more you lay still and rest your body, the faster your body parts will heal."

I asked, "Which body parts?"

She counted the injuries on the fingers of her left hand. "A dislocated left shoulder, a slightly cracked rib, and a small hairline fracture of your left hip all due to your slamming sideways into the car door, armrest, and handle when the airbag deployed. And let's not leave out a mild concussion, bruises, contusions, and topical burns from the airbag. I'd hold off on running any marathons for a few weeks. Otherwise, you're in tip-top shape."

Who says doctors lack a sense of humor?

I smirked. "Another item on my bucket list of things I wanted to experience. Now I can cross it off."

She waggled a finger and tsked. "Sarcasm is such an unbecoming character trait."

Before I could deliver the snappy retort sitting on the tip of my tongue, there was a knock on the door. Detective Jones and a fatigued Miguel Martinez—holding a gorgeous bouquet of daisies in the crook of his arm—came into the room. Miguel's normal olive complexion had turned as gray as wet cement. All things considered, he looked a lot worse than me.

Jones said, "Good morning Ms. Schlivnik."

I said, "Good morning, gentlemen. To what do I owe the pleasure of your company—business or pleasure?"

Jones smiled tightly. "Regrettably, for business. If you're up to it, we need to ask you some questions."

Snip put the instruments back in her medical bag and gave them a stern lecture. "She's still pretty weak. Don't overdo it. You may need to come back for her to finish the interview."

Snip patted a love tap on my cheek and slid into her jacket. "I'll be back as soon as my shift is over." She closed her medical bag, grabbed her purse, and waved goodbye. "Try not to get into any more trouble between now and then."

I fired back. "Try to improve your bedside manner between now and then."

She held out her palms. "My patients never complain."

I rolled my eyes and laughed. "Dead men tell no tales."

My favorite coroner grinned and gave me the middle finger salute as she walked out the door.

The two cops situated themselves on uncomfortable-looking straight-backed plastic chairs they pulled from the corner of the room and placed on each side of the bed.

Miguel bussed my cheek and laid the bouquet of daisies in my lap as he gave me the once-over. "How are you feeling?"

I smiled sardonically. "Probably better than I look."

Jones took a small tape recorder out of a messenger bag. "You sure you're up to doing this now? It's always best to get a witness's statement as close to the episode as possible, while it's still fresh in their mind." He held his hands out as though fending off a punch. "But Sophie Cutler will serve my head on a platter if we do this before you're ready."

I said, "I doubt I'll *ever forget* a single detail. Since you're already here, let's give it a whirl. I'll tell you if I need to stop."

Jones nodded and turned on the tape recorder. "Can you tell us what happened?"

"I was driving north on Coldwater Canyon right after dark into the valley to meet my friend Chris at the Encino Hills Fashion Galleria. As I drove past The Canyon Market, a car going way too fast for a two-lane mountain road pulled up behind me and flashed his lights for me to let him pass. I pulled over to the right as far as possible and flashed my brights for him to go around me. Instead of passing me, he flashed the brights again and blasted his horn. I've no idea what he expected me to do. It was too curvy a road to safely speed up. There was no verge between the cliff and the pavement, so I had no place to go. We came around a curve and the lunatic rammed his car into my bumper."

Jones asked, "You get a look at the car from your rearview mirror?"

Surely you jest, Detective.

"Honestly, I was too busy trying to maintain control of the car to look. Even if I did, it was too dark to get a good look at the vehicle. From the strength of the jolt, this was either an SUV or a pickup."

Jones and Miguel shared an uninterpretable look. Curious.

Jones asked, "What happened next?"

"I misjudged the angle of the next turn and hit the brake too hard as the car careened around the curve. As we came into the center of curvature, the maniac rammed my bumper with so much force that my car skidded into a hard right toward the side of the sheer cliff. I managed to stay in control of the car. Then I ran out of road. The lunatic *rammed me again*. The rental shimmied and fishtailed off the pavement into a shallow layer of gravel then slammed into the runaway truck berm at the edge of the cliff."

Miguel made a sour face and pressed his lips into a thin line. "It's a miracle you weren't killed."

Jones asked, "From your position, could you see what happened to the other car?"

I nodded. "The guy lost control of his car. It clipped the end of the berm and spun around to the precipice."

My eyes filled. "I suppose momentum took control and it sailed over the edge of the cliff." I pointed to the room. "Then I woke up here to Snip poking and prodding me."

I held my breath after I inquired. "And the other guy?"

Jones clasped his hands together as if in prayer. "He didn't make it. After Mr. Hancock's vehicle went over the cliff, it caromed off a rocky ledge, plunged to the bottom of the crevice, and exploded upon impact."

My eyes bugged. "*Mr. Hancock*? As in Sharon Hancock's *ex-husband*?"

Jones nodded. "Yes. *That* Mr. Hancock."

I narrowed my eyes. "If the car exploded, the driver's body got incinerated. Why are you convinced it was him?"

Jones said, "The rear license plate wasn't destroyed. We ran the plate through DMV and found the name of who the vehicle was registered to."

I said, "Just because the vehicle is registered to Mr. Hancock, doesn't mean he drove the car last night."

Jones nodded. "You're right. Once we found the vehicle registration information, we requested Mr. Hancock's dentist provide the coroner's office with the victim's dental records. Dr. Cutler compared his dental records to the corpse and made a positive ID."

Good grief, what if the children were with him?

I gasped, "Was he alone?"

Jones nodded. "Yes."

Thank the Goddess. I released the breath I didn't realize I'd held.

My heart ached for Sharon's poor babies. In less than a week, they became orphans. But at least they were alive.

I said, "Talk about a small world…"

Miguel pursed his lips. "This is no coincidence. You were a *target*."

I poked my index finger into my cleavage. "Why me? I barely knew him."

Miguel snapped, "Dear God, please don't tell me you *questioned him* regarding his ex-wife being involved in Mrs. Waxman's murder!"

I rolled my eyes. "No...I wish I had." I laughed. "You give me too much credit for sleuthing."

Miguel asked, "Were you a client?"

I slammed the bouquet of daisies on the bed. "Good grief! *Certainly not*. We met *coincidentally*. While waiting for Queenie, I ran into Sharon at Coast Burgers in the marina one night. She was waiting for her ex to bring their children for a supervised visit. When he and the kids arrived, Sharon introduced us, and then I left them to meet Queenie waiting at our table."

Jones asked, "*That's it*, Ms. Schlivnik?"

I grimaced as I tried to hold out my hands. "Yes, for crying out loud! *That's it*. Only the *one time*."

Miguel drummed his fingers on the bed's metal guard rail. "One time. Doesn't add up to attempting vehicular manslaughter."

"Just because I met him one brief time doesn't mean I was a target. Why was he in such a hurry to get over the hill? Maybe his kids were in the valley for some reason and he was late picking them up. Why can't it be only a coincidence I had the misfortune of not moving fast enough to suit him? Why must it be I was a specific target?"

As I asked the question, even I didn't believe it.

Miguel said, "Because the lab examined your rental car and they found a *tracking device* attached to your muffler. The tracker bore Mr. Hancock's fingerprints on it. *That's why*. The important question to ask is *why did he track your car*?"

"No idea," I smirked, "*You're the detective...you tell me*."

Jones turned off the tape recorder and packed it back in his messenger bag. He stood. "Thank you, Ms.

Schlivnik for giving us your statement. I'll get it typed and you can review and sign it once you're up and around."

Jones turned to Miguel. "I'll meet you back at the cop shop later."

The detective lumbered across the room as though he carried a heavy burden. He opened the door and turned to face us. "I hope your recovery is a swift one, Ms. Schlivnik."

Once Jones left, Miguel took the bouquet off the bed and motioned to the door. "I better ask the nurse for something to put these in. They'll last a lot longer in water." Concerned about the flowers or need an excuse to escape? Miguel made a face like he needed to fart when I motioned to the phone. "Nurse's station is extension 326."

Nice try, Mickey.

A volunteer brought a large water-filled ceramic vase and arranged the flowers in it. She put the vase on the table next to the bed and asked if I needed anything else. I said no, and she wished me a speedy recovery as she walked out of the room.

Miguel squirmed in the chair next to the bed, unable to find a place for himself. He fidgeted with his tie for something to do with his hands. As though he drew a blank for anything meaningful to say, he inanely asked, "So, how are you doing?"

I clucked my tongue. "We already covered the subject. What's the real reason you are here? Certainly not to conduct a witness interview. That is your detective's job. I'm in no mood for one of your lectures. If you have something to say, spit it out already. If not, I'm exhausted, so, please let yourself out."

The words stuck in his mouth as he choked them out. "W-why e-else? I-I've b-been f-frantic at the t-thought of l-losing y-you."

He slammed his fist on the metal tray next to the bed. "I've begged, pleaded, cajoled, threatened—short of locking you up, I've done everything possible to stop you from interfering in our cases. And I've failed miserably."

He held out his hands in supplication. "You win. I give up. You'll *never* stop."

I tried to argue, but the words died in my throat. How could I stop? As if I had a choice. It's not in my DNA.

He hovered his index finger over his thumb to drive home his point. "Every time you've stuck your nose into one of our investigations, you've come this close to getting yourself killed." His eyes filled. "I love you, but I can't continue to live in constant fear that the next call I get concerning your welfare will be from the morgue, not a hospital. I'm sorry. I just can't do this anymore."

He sighed and leaned over the bed rail to gently brush his lips on my forehead. Without waiting for a response, Miguel Martinez walked out the door and out of my life.

Chapter Thirty-Two

They say sleep is the best medicine. Regrettably, an endless parade of visitors prevented the prescription from getting filled. I appreciated everyone's concern, however, the only way I'd get any rest was when the doctor released me after a two-day hospital stay.

Considering the grocery list of injuries I sustained, I was doing pretty darn well. Fortunately, none of my injuries required surgery. The doctor rotated my arm back into place so while still temporarily in a sling, my dislocated shoulder is back in the socket where it belongs.

For the cracked rib, the doctor instructed me to take ibuprofen for any pain and to hold an ice pack wrapped in a towel on the affected rib every few hours for the first few days to bring down the swelling.

The small hairline fracture on my hip was due to extreme force from the accident. The ends of the fractured bone were impacted or pushed together. The doctor said this type of fracture would heal naturally without surgery. I will be using a cane for a few months and won't be driving for a couple of weeks.

The swelling of my lips has gone down considerably and the shiner will fade away in a week or two. The burns from the airbag are almost all healed.

I looked forward to getting home and back to my normal routine. Regrettably, my Uncle Barry shot the concept to smithereens. To prevent my mother from taking the first flight to LA and moving me lock, stock, and barrel to Miami, I had to accept a deal with my dad's baby brother: He would not reveal the circumstances of *how* I sustained the injuries to my parents *only* if I agreed to move into his Beverly Hills home for the duration of my recovery.

When he first proposed the arrangement, fiercely independent me, fought it tooth and nail. "My injuries aren't serious. No surgeries. They look worse than they are. If you don't take my word for it, ask my doctor friend Sophie Cutler."

He speared me with an evil smile. "Nope. My proposal is a take-it-as-is-or-leave-it proposition."

He laughed in my face when I said, "You're a *lawyer*. Didn't your law school teach you that *blackmail is illegal?*"

Uncle Barry clucked his tongue. "Blackmail is such an ugly word. Besides," He said, "I'm not blackmailing you. Every action gets a reaction. I'm merely explaining *what my* reaction to *your* action would be."

After several rounds of lively negotiations, I finally got him down from two weeks to one. The futility of further arguing became crystal clear. I proved no match for him. No wonder they call him Savage Schlivnik around legal circles. Once we resolved my recovery site, I arranged for Siggie to stay at AJ's so my overly affectionate pooch couldn't knock me over by accident.

Uncle Barry's long-time housekeeper Conchita sprang into action to prepare my uncle's house for my one-week stay. Even though ambulatory, my going up and down stairs to reach the guest bedroom would not be a brain surgeon move. By the time Uncle Barry brought me home, Conchita had the downstairs den set up as my bedroom and office. My clothes hung in the closet, my shoes on the closet floor, and my undies and socks in the top desk drawer. And thanks to Harriet, my laptop and important files waited for me on the desk.

What a week. Restaurant-quality meals that were served on fancy China three times a day. Aquatic exercises in an Olympic-sized pool. Sleeping in. Somebody else making the bed. A girl could get used to this. This wasn't a recovery. More like a working vacation. So much for my negotiation prowess. If I realized there'd be such a level of pampering, forget two weeks—I should have insisted on a month.

****

One Week Later:

Living in the lap of luxury had been a treat. Yet as wise-beyond-her-years Dorothy Gale of the Wizard of Oz fame once said, *there's no place like home.* Buddy picked me up at Uncle Barry's, then we went to AJ's house to retrieve my hound. Siggie was overjoyed to see me. AJ, Miguel's greatest fan gave me the cold shoulder.

After Buddy hauled all my stuff from Uncle Barry's onto the boat, we shared a takeaway pizza, a bottle of wine, and the promise of tomorrow.

We finished eating and washed the dishes. Buddy opened the cabinet to put the dishes inside and noticed my nana's brass Shabbos Candlesticks on the bottom shelf. He fingered the treasured heirloom. "These are the same kind of candlesticks my mee-maw lights and says a prayer over on Friday night."

I took them down from the shelf, turned them upside down, and Buddy stood next to me as I traced the inlaid inscription on the bottoms. *Warszawa March 26,1897*

Shmuel (Samuel) and Fruma (Fannie) Harpinski

"These candlesticks were a wedding gift from my great-great-grandparents to my nana's mother and father. They have an amazing story. My great-grandparents lived in a Jewish Shtetl ghetto-style village across the river from Warsaw. Theirs was an arranged marriage. Once they married, things became much worse for Polish Jews. After one of the bloodier pogroms, my great-grandparents decided to leave Poland via the Jewish underground. This was a network of brave souls throughout Eastern Europe who helped Jews escape. My great-grandfather was a tailor and he went first. He made his way north to Birmingham, England, and took a job sewing the coal miners' uniforms. He saved his money, and after two years, he sent for my great-grandmother. She received word to be ready quickly." My voice caught. "Imagine saying goodbye to your parents, siblings, and friends, and realizing you might *never* see them again?"

Wide-eyed, Buddy shook his head.

"Anyway," I continued, "A man came to their shtetel at midnight on a moonless night. One small knapsack that held a change of clothes, a family photo, and these candlesticks were all my great-grandmother could take. She bid her family goodbye, and the man took her to the narrowest part of the wide Warsaw River, infamous for its dangerously strong currents. If you were unfamiliar with the way they ran, you'd be pulled under by the current and drown. My great-grandmother climbed on the man's back, and he swam her across. On the other side, he handed her to the next underground person. She slept in forests and caves during the days and traveled either by horseback or on foot at night. It took her over two months to travel this way across Europe. She arrived at Calais and boarded a freighter to England, and finally reunited with my great-grandfather."

Buddy whistled. "Your great-grandparents' story is amazing. It could be a movie." He mused, "Mee-maw's candlesticks must have a story too. I aim to find out what it is."

After we cleaned up the galley, we took our wine onto the aft deck. We toasted one another and given the events of the last couple of weeks, *L'Chaim: Yiddish for To Life* could never be more meaningful.

I put a CD of a Brazilian saxophonist into the player. We sat next to one another in deck chairs and held hands watching the cerulean ocean swallow the fiery orange sun. As the CD cut to the artist's most popular tune, Buddy drew me out of my chair and into his embrace. The steady beat of his heart kept time against my breasts. He held me carefully so as not to worsen my injuries while we danced slowly around the deck. My eyes filled as his voice dropped low and husky when he whispered into my hair, "*This* is where you belong."

Nana's voice talked inside my head.

One door closes, another one opens.

Chapter Thirty-Three

The normalcy of the morning Yenta coffee klatch and challenges at work brought life back into its proper perspective. Queenie chauffeured me to and from the office until my doctor cleared me to drive. The following Monday morning she dropped me off at Johnny's. I celebrated the reunion with my beloved convertible by dropping the top and taking a glorious drive along Pacific Coast Highway.

While I recovered at Uncle Barry's, Detective Jones released Gary from jail. Something finally convinced stubborn-as-a-mule Josiah Jones that Sharon killed Leni and then herself, so no one else had been arrested. Good news, bad news.

While I'd made a concerted effort to put the nightmare of the Waxman-Hancock debacle behind me, I fought a losing battle. I still had an itch to scratch. Tuesday night I brewed a pot of coffee and spread the photos from Sharon's apartment across the galley table. I stared at the photo of the coffee cup and saucer in the kitchen sink all night to no avail. My gut said Leni and Sharon's murders are linked…if I could only figure out how.

Wednesday morning, I bent over to retrieve a fabric swatch that fell out of a presentation folder, and something pulled in my left thigh up to my hip. Crap. Please, Goddess, don't let my stupidity worsen the hairline fracture. I needed another hospital visit like I needed a migraine. I used the cane and hobbled around in pain all day.

****

Snip and I made dinner plans for that same night. We hadn't seen one another since I was in the hospital. Maybe she could take a look at my hip? For once in my life, neither a burger nor pizza rang my chimes. A new Thai restaurant opened two months ago three doors down from Coast Burgers on the north side of the Washington Street Pier. Queenie and I tried unsuccessfully to get in the first few weeks after the opening. I don't care how great the reviews were in *The Argonaut*—our local Marina throwaway paper. *No place* is worth a three-hour wait.

I suggested we see if the intrigue of Bangkok at the Beach had subsided by now, and Snip was game. For a Wednesday night, the place was busy, but fortunately, there was no wait for a table.

Lush tropical décor accented by pastel colors was easy on the eyes. The hostess guided us to a cozy booth for two. A bamboo table divided the floral print cushioned bench seats angled to face the ocean.

The waiter left after we ordered and Snip gave me the once over. "All things considered you look remarkably well."

I grimaced as I stood and leaned on the cane.

She eyed me up and down. "You're limping."

"This morning, I bent over to pick up a fabric swatch on the floor and I hurt all day. Do you think I worsened the fracture on my hip?"

She gestured to my left leg. "Where does it hurt?"

I grazed my fingers over my left thigh.

Snip rolled her eyes. "I guess you flunked physiology. For crying out loud, can't you tell the difference between *your thigh and your hip*? Your *hip* isn't damaged. If you widened the fracture beyond a hairline, you'd be in intense pain and hardly able to walk. You pulled a *thigh muscle*. It'll be uncomfortable for a couple of days and then it will be fine. In the future, bend using the ballerina stance the way the physical therapist taught you and you won't be in danger of further injuring the hip."

"Are you sure it isn't the hip?"

She rolled her eyes. "I'm a doctor. We studied this stuff in med school. I am on pretty secure ground here."

Snip indelicately snorted when I burst off-key into song. "*The hip bone's connected to the thigh bone.*"

Snip arched a brow. "Take my advice and keep your day job."

I gave my favorite forensic the middle finger salute and sat down as the waiter arrived to serve our wine. He filled two glasses halfway up and we raised ours in a toast. "L'Chaim."

She glugged a gulp and said with not a scintilla of irony, "You came a little too close to becoming one of my patients, and this time you paid one helluva high price." Snip pursed her lips. "Miguel Martinez is as fine a man as you'll ever meet. And he's crazy for you—why I'll never know. You blew it big this time, Hol."

Fanfreakingtastic. A lecture from another charter member of the Martinez fan club.

I held my hands out. "It was *inevitable*. Miguel and I have been on a collision course for a while now." I shrugged. "Just like my nana would say in Yiddish—it wasn't bershert—not meant to be. The ironic thing is *this time* I wasn't the instigator."

Snip scratched the crown of her hair. "Meaning?"

"Meaning I never contacted Hancock for *anything*, let alone question him." I pointed to the restaurant a few doors down. "I ran into Sharon at the pier location of Coast Burgers. We chatted while waiting for the arrival of our dinner partners. I met the ex-husband *once* for two minutes. Sharon introduced us when he brought their children to the restaurant for a supervised visit with their mother. I said *nice to meet you* to the guy and went to my table to wait for Queenie."

Snip grinned. "You made one helluva first impression on him. Imagine what more he'd do if you'd stayed to chat and turned on the Schlivnik charm?"

I made a sour face. "Funny. Not. That brief interaction wasn't the catalyst for him to go after me."

Snip pursed her lips. "Well, you did *something* to piss the guy off enough to want to kill you. Any idea what you did?"

I nodded. "Yeah. I do. Remember, we found out he and Barry Waxman were law partners." I held my hands out like a movie director posing a scene. "Try this on for size: Barry Waxman tells Hancock you've subpoenaed his and Hadassah's fingerprints. That the Waxmans are fighting it *screams* they have something to hide. Hadassah tells her brother that I overheard Sharon at the Bainbridge buyer's office dissing Rapido to the buyer. The Waxmans realize Sharon is playing them—a great motive to off her. They figure you're close to proving Sharon was murdered and didn't commit suicide. Barry tells all this to Hancock. Maybe Hancock discovers Sharon's best friend and the Godmother of their children *is my cousin.* Hancock figures out I am the one feeding you the information. In the interim, Sharon secures pro bono representation from the biggest Family Law firm in LA. Say G & G file something at the court to stop Hancock from taking Sharon's kids to San Diego. Hancock is served and goes berserk. Say Hancock goes to Sharon's on the pretext of making a deal. However, his real intention is to kill her. The Waxman docs and the suicide note were typed on the same machine. If the machine is in Waxman and Hancock's law office, and their fingerprints are on all the documents and the suicide note, it's enough to make an arrest. Hancock panics when he sees Detective Jones at Sharon's funeral and figures you'll subpoena his fingerprints next. I'd bet my boat Hancock's fingerprints are the ones on the suicide note and the cup and saucer Janie and I found in Sharon's apartment."

Snip wrinkled her brow. "I counted enough ifs and maybes in your scenario to sink your houseboat. Even if all your supposition is right, it still doesn't explain him going after *you*."

Good grief.

"Have you been inhaling too much of the formaldehyde?" I gave her the big eyes. "*Of course, it explains it*. Hancock murdered Sharon and *I'm the one* who has been helping you prove it."

Snip clucked her tongue. "And forcing you over a cliff would help him how?"

I grinned. "Dead men tell no tales."

I waggled my fingers in the air. "Snip, humor me and compare the fingerprints on the suicide note and the cup and saucer in Sharon's sink to Hancock's fingerprints. Detective Jones said the police got Mr. Hancock's prints off a tracking device he put on my rental car." I clasped my hands together as though in prayer. "Sharon Hancock's children just lost both of their parents. If I'm right, their father murdered their mother. You can't bring their parents back to them, at least you can provide these orphans with the solace their mother left them involuntarily."

Chapter Thirty-Four

Snip called the next afternoon to say I was right—
the fingerprints on the suicide note and the cup and
saucer matched those of Sharon's ex-husband. Should I
be gratified or horrified? Maybe a little of both. Proving
Sharon's ex-husband murdered her unfortunately didn't
change the outcome, still, it would give those who cared
about her a measure of closure.

One murder was solved. One remained a mystery. I
only knew Leni Waxman by reputation until Gary got
arrested for her murder. So, at the risk of sounding
heartless, my reaction to her demise was one of those
"*Gee, isn't that awful*" moments when you need to say
something. You might even wonder whodunit, then you
shrug it off and go on living your life. I only started my
investigation into Leni's murder to prove my partner's
innocence in committing the crime. After Gary's
exoneration, the smart money said to quit while you're
ahead. As I've always stated, no one ever confused me
with Albert Einstein.

Somebody poisoned Leni Waxman. Since Gary
didn't do it, who did? I'd still bet my boat Sharon was
the guilty party. And if I were right, some folks would
say Sharon paid the ultimate price for her crime and close
the book on Leni Waxman's murder. I'd disagree. If
Sharon killed Leni, she deserved to be judged by a jury
of her peers, not by one person appointing themselves

judge, jury, and executioner.

Yet this wasn't my fight, so it begged the question of why I couldn't let this one go. The answer? Love her or loathe her, Leni Waxman deserved justice. Sounds good, right? The truth? This was one mystery I *had to solve* or I'd never enjoy another moment's peace.

I still had a great deal of work to do in preparation for an upcoming presentation for Sue Ellen Magee that was due in only two days. Try as I might to complete the prep work, my mind wandered back to Leni Waxman's killer. Questions of whodunit ran a continuous loop through my addled mind all day.

What do the cops always say on TV? *Follow the money.*

What does Queenie always ask? *Who had the most to lose?*

What did I learn the hard way to ask? *Who had the most to gain?*

Who benefitted most from Leni dying?

Who benefitted most from Gary's arrest?

Who benefitted most from vandalizing my car?

Who benefitted most by stopping my investigation?

Who benefitted most from Sharon Hancock's murder?

No matter which path I traveled down, all roads led to only one person.

Holy guacamole.

I dialed Detective Jones's office number, and the call went directly to voicemail. I left a message and called Miguel next, and got the same zip-o-de-do-dah result for my trouble. Who am I kidding? After washing his hands of me, I had a better chance of winning the lottery than Miguel Martinez *ever* returning one of my calls.

For someone who had a precinct full of law enforcement contacts, I was running out of names. This next one was at best a long shot, but the clock was ticking. I dialed LAPD homicide detective AJ Yakamura's cell phone and crossed my fingers that she'd pick up. Of course, after the cold shoulder she gave me over my breakup with Miguel it came as no surprise AJ didn't answer my calls.

The detectives under Miguel's command were a tight-knit group. While she wasn't involved in the case, no doubt Glory Washington heard an earful by now about my interference antics from Miguel and Detective Jones. Should I call her? What did I have to lose? The phone rang and rang. No surprise. I didn't need practice dialing a phone, so no sense in calling her partner. I crossed Glory and Gator Goodwin off my mental list.

The odds they're *all* out of the office at the same time? Slimsky to nonesky. The more likely scenario? I'd pissed them all off big time, and they're not taking my calls. Fanfreakingtastic. I've got a killer to catch and most of the Rampart Station cops were too angry at me to respond to my calls.

Out of desperation, I dialed Snip at the office as well as on her cell. My calls to her also went to voicemail. I left a message asking her to pass along my messages to the cops, which even to my ears, bordered on hysterical. I prayed she listened to her voicemail a lot more often than I do mine.

When or *if would* one of them will *ever* return my call? I couldn't sit around forever with my thumb up my ass waiting. They all can't avoid me forever—could they? *Not if I don't let them.* There was only one thing left to do. Camp out at the Rampart Station and make a complete pest of myself until one of the cops listens to me.

Chapter Thirty-Five

I stepped out of the Apparel Mart parking structure elevator and turned the corner to get to my car. I stopped short and shoved a fist in my mouth to stifle a scream. Wide-eyed from fear, Barry Waxman faced Hadassah, who aimed the business end of a revolver at her brother's head. Barry faced me. Fortunately, Hadassah's back was to me. I made a shushing sign with my index finger and prayed Barry got the message and didn't react.

Venomous rage dripped from her tone as Hadassah snarled. "You high and mighty arrogant jerk. Always acting like you're so much smarter than me. You're nothing more than a self-righteous punk in an expensive business suit. First, you lied about the instructions Mom gave you to change her will, and then you dared to confront me regarding any role I may or may not have played in her death."

Hadassah's evil laugh terrified me to the core. "If *any two* deserved what they got, it is your *precious mother* and that loser Sharon Hancock. You *actually thought* I'd let you turn *your sister* into the cops *and not pay a price?*"

Barry's hands shook as he held them out in supplication yet his voice stayed remarkably calm. "First of all, I never said I would turn you over to the authorities. I told you to *turn yourself in*. It's the only way to cut a deal. I'm a lawyer. No need for me to turn you in. Take it from me. The cops start nosing around when too many bodies start piling up near you."

I beg to differ, Counselor. So far, they've done everything but...

Barry jutted his jaw. "Secondly, I didn't lie. Even though she is *our mother*, attorney-client privilege *prohibited me* from revealing the details of Mother's will until it went into probate." Barry's eyes darkened. "Now the truth is out. We weren't cut out of her estate. She didn't leave the company to the hospital. She left it to *us*. Congratulations, genius. You murdered our mother for nothing."

Good gravy, Barry. Dial it down a few notches. That's no water pistol she's aiming at your head.

If I had a brain, I'd have run for my life. Instead, I stood rooted to the spot, intent on listening to these two idiots pointing fingers at one another.

Hadassah shook with fury. "You call that the truth? Ha. Mother promised to *retire and relinquish her duties to me* the day I turned twenty-five and that in five years all ownership of the company reverted to *me*. She reneged on her promise on my twenty-fifth spouting some BS that I wasn't ready to take over the reins. I turned *thirty* in November and she still sang the same old song." Hadassah pursed her lips. "She n*ever* intended relinquishing responsibility to anyone else—especially *me*. If I didn't do something, she would continue making excuse after excuse to hold onto the company until she died—probably keel over while tracing a pattern at the cutting table."

Hadassah cocked the gun and Barry's voice cracked. "For God's sake, Hadassah! Please. I just asked Deborah to marry me and she said yes. I finally became a full partner at my firm. I have my whole life ahead of me. Please don't do this. Let's work this out."

Hadassah clucked her tongue. "As usual, *everything must always be about you. Not this time, bro.*" She sighted the gun and aimed for the spot right between Barry's eyes.

So much for brotherly love.

Barry pled for his life. "*Please Hadassah.* I'm begging you."

Attaboy, keep her talking, I prayed Barry got my telepathic message.

I had to do something. But what? I was in no condition for heroics. A distraction? Then what? Hadassah shoots us both? Face it, Schlivnik, you couldn't do anything on your own. I needed help. A quick look around. Nada. Naturally, whenever you need someone, there isn't a soul on the whole damned floor.

The guard shack wasn't far—about halfway from the elevators in the back corner. Of course, with my handicap, it might as well be on Mars. Was a guard even there? What if it was Ernesto, the hunched-over, ancient security guard? By the time the old guy shuffled back here, Barry would probably be dead. But beggars couldn't be choosers. The old man had a walkie-talkie and could radio for help. The old buzzard was my only hope. In the best of times, with my short legs, I was no speed walker. With the added attraction of hobbling around with a cane, could I even get to the guard shack in time? There was no other option. I had to at least try.

As I backed away, the heel of my shoe caught on the edge of the indoor/outdoor carpet draped in front of the elevator bank. I tripped and whacked my cane into the metal trash container placed between the two elevators while trying to keep my balance. I tottered precariously with my ass ending up on the rim of the container, but by some miracle, I didn't fall in.

Hadassah turned sideways at the clash of two metals. The sight of me with my ass half in the trashcan sent her into hysterics. "If it isn't little Miss Persistent." My blood ran cold as she mused, "You had a helluva good run. Too bad your luck finally ran out."

Hadassah waved the gun at Barry. "Don't move a muscle. Don't so much as fart or I'll lower my aim and shoot your nuts off for fun before I finish you off."

Yikes.

My cell phone rang. Could it finally be the cops? Better late than never. Nah. Who was I kidding? With my luck, it was probably some jerk dialing the wrong number trying to order a pizza. Before I could hit the talk button, Hadassah smacked the phone out of my hand with the barrel of the gun. The phone hit the ground and broke into a bazillion pieces after she stomped on it with the heel of her shoe. I doubted the warranty covered this.

Hadassah waved the gun toward Barry. "Get next to Perry Mason and let's get this thing done."

I used my cane for leverage and hoisted myself up. I hobbled next to Barry. Any chance of talking my way out of this catastrophe slipped away as Hadassah dismissed it with a sweep of the gun. Her eyes turned hard as granite. "Your meddling got your car vandalized. Your interference got Sharon killed. If you didn't keep sticking your nose where it didn't belong, you wouldn't be involved in all this. But no, you just couldn't let it go. I warned you over and over, yet you paid my warnings no attention." She lectured, "You should have listened and taken the hint. You didn't, and this is where it brought you to." She jerked her head at Barry and spat. "Now you're another loose end to tie up along with *him*."

As Hadassah moved closer to reduce the distance between us to point-blank range, she cocked the hammer and aimed the gun between her brother's eyes.

And I was next. My knees threatened to buckle as I looked certain death in the eye. I leaned against an Italian luxury sportscar parked on the other side of my convertible for support and the car alarm screamed a pulsating, high-pitched whine.

Hadassah instinctively turned toward the noise. Stubbornness and the will to live took over. While she was distracted, I two-handed my cane, miraculously still leashed to my wrist. I gripped the cane baseball bat-style. I ignored the excruciating pain in my shoulder and ribs as I wound up. I slammed the metal walking stick into Hadassah's midsection as hard as I could. The cane made a satisfyingly loud whoomph as it hit her in the breadbasket. All the air whooshed out of her lungs and she deflated like a leaky balloon. The momentum of the hit sent her pinwheeling and she cracked the side of her head on the concrete making a bone-jarring thud.

Hadassah dropped the gun as she fell. Remarkably it didn't go off when it hit the ground and bounced in front of me. Barry made a play for it, but I putted the gun golf-style with my cane away from his reach. I remembered to use the ballerina pose as I bent down to pick up the gun.

From here in the cheap seats, the guy seemed an innocent victim of circumstance. Yet the fact his sister was ready to blow his brains out five minutes ago might not matter to the man. Because either way—complicit or innocent—blood is still thicker than water. Could I trust him? Only one way to find out.

I pointed to his cell with the barrel of the gun. "Give me your phone."

He handed it over and I dialed nine-one-one. I gave our location and the Readers Digest version of events. I requested the operator to send an ambulance as well as the cops...and to please hurry.

I returned Barry's phone and motioned toward Hadassah's crumpled supine body. "Roll her over onto her stomach. Pull her arms behind her back and then cross her wrists one over the other and keep her hands flat against her back. Hold her arms tight. Sit on her back if need be, just don't let her move a muscle if she wakes up." I pointed to my car. "I'll be back."

I hobbled to the convertible and opened the trunk. I grabbed a set of bungee cords and limped back to the Waxmans. Barry and I traded places.

I shoved the gun into my pants pocket and handed my cane to Barry to free up my hands and then leaned on him for support. I bent Hadassah's rubbery legs back at the knees and pulled them to her pliable arms. I used the first bungee cord to hogtie her wrists and ankles together in tight sailor reef square knots. She could writhe and wiggle around forever, but she'd never get loose. I wound the second bungee around her body and bound Hadassah in a butterfly loop. After I finished trussing her, she resembled a cross between a Thanksgiving turkey ready for the oven and a lassoed rodeo calf.

Chapter Thirty-Six

I eased my weary bones into my usual seat at the Yenta table and gratefully accepted my cuppa from Hope. The latest edition of The West Coast Apparel News was spread across the middle of the table. I cringed at the boldface headline above the fold: *M3 Schools LAPD Again*

Good gravy. If Miguel hadn't already dumped me, that headline would no doubt have done the trick.

The Yentas raised their coffee cups in a salute.

Joan tapped a spoon over the headline and grinned. "Our own Mart Murder Magnet has done it again."

I poked my index finger into my cleavage. "*Trust me, I schooled no one.* This is merely a case of being in the *wrong place at the right time.*"

Sonia wagged her index finger at me. "Don't sell yourself short, Nancy Drew. As I recall, you pegged Sharon for Leni's murder from day one. And *once again, the cops got it wrong.*"

I nodded. "Yes, I got it right. But this whole sordid mess turned out to be a lot more complicated than your average run-of-the-mill murder. I had all the pieces to the puzzle but no clue how they all fit together. Thanks to Barry Waxman's help, here's all I've been able to piece together: If you recall, according to Hadassah, Leni promised to turn over running Rapido to her on her daughter's twenty-fifth birthday. When the time came,

Leni reneged on the vow saying Hadassah wasn't ready to take the reins. And five years later, Leni still refused to give up control. Hadassah figured Leni would *never live up to her vow* and took things into her own hands…"

Queenie's tone rose to an incredulous squeal. "Good grief! Are you saying Hadassah *murdered her mother* because she *welched on a deal?*"

I nodded. "Yeah. Hadassah decided to get rid of her mother but she had no workable game plan in mind. After Leni fired Sharon Hancock and blackballed her in the industry, Hadassah realized Sharon could be a willing accomplice. When she learned Sharon attended nursing school and possessed a knowledge of poisons, Hadassah approached Sharon with a proposition: If Sharon murdered Leni, Hadassah would take over Rapido and make Sharon the company's Executive Vice President and give her a minority interest in the firm. Sharon agreed and did her part. The police found a vial of nicotine, surgical gloves, and a paintbrush hidden in the well of the trunk of Sharon's car."

Hope asked, "How did Sharon get into the ballroom before the party?"

I said, "The cops surmised she snuck in with the catering team. But Sharon didn't trust Hadassah, so she hedged her bet by accepting Allen Brown's job offer. As it turned out, Sharon's hunch proved right. Hadassah lived up to her pledge to make Sharon the company EVP but reneged on the ownership part of the deal."

I tipped my head. "I guess Sharon figured turnaround is fair play because while she and Hadassah negotiated, she neglected to share she'd been working for Allen since before the Hanukkah party."

My smile dimmed. "Here's the role I inadvertently

played: When I met Hadassah for coffee, I commented she had made a lot of changes at Rapido in a short period. I mentioned one of my colleagues observed her and her brother going over documents with Sharon. Those docs turned out to be the deal Hadassah and Sharon negotiated. I asked her about Sharon, and Hadassah told me about the offer. She said barring complications, the deal would be finalized by the end of the week. I told her about Sharon and Allen trying to sandbag Rapido and Hadassah said Sharon would *regret her decision*. By revealing to Hadassah Sharon's double-cross I probably got Sharon and her ex-husband killed."

Hope wrinkled her brow. "How does *that* make you responsible for the Hancocks' deaths?"

I held out my hands. "If I never told Hadassah about Sharon's double cross, she wouldn't have discussed it with her brother and his law partner—who turned out to be Sharon's ex-husband. Around the same time as this happened, Sharon's ex announced he received a promotion to run the new office in San Diego and would be moving with Sharon's children to La Jolla. Sharon hired a powerful Family Law firm to prevent him from taking the kids out of LA County. Barry told me Sharon's ex-husband went berserk after being served with court papers. He contacted Hadassah and they conspired to kill Sharon. Hadassah is a gardener and gave the ex-husband the weed killer to poison Sharon. He went to Sharon's house under the pretext of working out a child custody deal. His real intention was to kill her and he succeeded."

Sonia pointed to my cane. "I still don't understand why the ex-husband came after you."

I shrugged. "I guess he and Hadassah compared

notes and figured out I was the one who fed Snip all the information. After Snip subpoenaed the Waxman's fingerprints, Hadassah got nervous and made Barry fight the court order. She and Sharon's ex saw Detective Jones at Sharon's funeral and the ex-husband probably figured he was next."

Joan gave me the kindergarten teacher's look of disapproval over the rims of her glasses. "And running you over a cliff helped him how?"

I laughed. "Snip made the same observation. I'll tell you the same thing I said to her. Dead men tell no tales."

I sighed. "When Leni said Hadassah wasn't ready to take over the company and refused to relinquish control of Rapido, she also told Hadassah she made changes to her will. Much to Hadassah's frustration, Leni refused to reveal the changes. Hadassah assumed Leni welched on their deal because she decided to leave Rapido to the hospital and cut her family out of the will. That's why Hadassah set the wheels in motion to murder Leni before the new will could be put into place. Barry drew up Leni's revised will. Hadassah demanded Barry reveal the changes. Despite her being family, because of client-attorney privilege, Barry refused to tell Hadassah until Leni approved and signed the updated will. As it turned out, Leni left Rapido to Hadassah and Barry."

Hope's jaw dropped. "So, Hadassah killed Leni for nothing."

Joan funneled her lips. "Her mother had it right about her daughter after all."

I said, "Barry figured out Hadassah set up Leni's murder and told her to turn herself in. That's when she pulled the gun on him and the rest is history."

Sonia asked, "What happens to Rapido now? Are

they going out of business? Or is it being sold"

I shook my head. "No. Barry went through Leni's old files and discovered proof that Allen Brown's allegation had been right all along—Leni stole Allen's idea. While both Barry and Hadassah inherited the company, it is illegal for her to financially benefit from her crime. Barry controls the company but he has no desire or expertise to run it. Rather than close Rapido down, Barry approached Allen with a proposition and Allen accepted. Barry and Allen merged their two companies. Allen will be the managing partner running the company and Barry will handle all the finances and legal work."

Joan lifted my cane and grinned. "You *used* this to subdue Hadassah?"

I nodded "Yeah. The cane and two bungee cords to truss her up until the cops arrived." I shrugged. "It was the only thing handy at the time. I hadn't *planned* to thwart her attempt to blow her brother's brains out. I was on my way to the Rampart precinct because *none of the cops including Miguel* answered my calls when I figured out Hadassah was responsible for Leni's murder. I got off the Mart parking structure elevator and discovered Hadassah pointing a gun at Barry's head."

Hope patted my arm. "You must be devastated by Miguel's breakup."

I twisted my hand back and forth. "Yes and no. Do I care for him? Yes. Deeply. Will I miss him? Absolutely. Did the breakup catch me by surprise? Not really. I'll tell you the same thing I told Snip. *It was inevitable.* Miguel and I have been on a collision course for a while now. *I am never going to change.* I know it. He knows it. And that turned out to be the deal-breaker for him." I shrugged. "As my nana said in Yiddish—some things are not bershert—not meant to be."

Queenie's eyes twinkled. "Since Buddy no longer has any competition, did your mother reserve the wedding venue?"

As I opened my mouth to make a snappy reply, the temperature dropped fifty degrees. I shivered and pulled my blazer tightly around my shoulders as the two spinning whirls of freezing air I'd become a tad too familiar with spun counterclockwise as twin tornados swirled down, and landed next to me.

Good gravy. Either news traveled at warp speed in the Great Beyond or my two favorite ghosts were stalking me. It could have gone either way.

Grinning from ear to ear, Marie and Justine LaValle bounced around like a couple of runaway beach balls and did their high-step version of the happy dance, replete with a synchronized wave and an ass-shaking hokey-pokey-style finale.

I bit my lower lip so hard not to laugh out loud that it's a wonder it didn't bleed.

Once they finished their routine, Marie put her thumb and index finger between her lips and blew out an ear-splitting victory whistle. If she wasn't already an apparition, her whistle would wake the dead. She raised her arms above her head and squealed, *"Praise Heaven above and Hallelujah! Our prayers have finally been answered."*

She skidded her palms across one another. "Ah say, goodbye and good riddance. It's about time the damned fool cop realized the error of his ways and said adios. What took him so long to figure out he had *no chance* of winning your hand *as long as I am around* is simply beyond me." She swiped her wrist across her forehead. "Thank the good Lord, ah kin stop givin' Mr. Po-liceman the evil eye day and night." She wagged her index finger at me. "Ah declare, that man is *almost as slow* on the uptake as you, and hand to God, Ah didn't think it possible."

Marie rubbed her hands together. "Well, as Mee-maw always said, the good Lord screwed our heads on lookin' forward for a reason." She clapped twice and grinned. "You better hustle your bustle Missy right fast, because we don't have a lot of time to make all them arrangements and a proper weddin' takes some plannin'."

Whoa. I better put the brakes on *this conversation* and pronto. I shook my head at Marie, but she didn't take the hint. If I didn't want to look like a crazy woman talking to the air, I needed to speak to the ghosts away from the Yentas' nosy ears. I held up my coffee cup and smiled sheepishly. "Little girl, little bladder. I'll be back in five minutes, and you guys can give me your fifty cents worth of opinion you're no doubt all dying to share."

The cane made an annoying clicking sound as I shuffled to the ladies' room diagonally across from the elevator bank in the mart lobby. I reached the door and prayed I'd find no one inside. I pulled open the handle and let out a sigh of relief. Praise the Goddess—nobody at the sinks and all the stall doors were open and empty.

The two ghosts floated through the door and followed me into the restroom.

Marie's icy glare froze me in my tracks. "What the Sam Hill are you talkin' about? Now that you're free of your *encumbrance*, we can proceed to the weddin'."

Marie crossed her arms over her chest and impatiently tapped a foot waiting for my answer.

I jutted my chin defiantly. "Hold on a Cincinnati minute, lady. We're a long way off, *if ever*, to making wedding plans."

Justine's lower lip trembled. "Why don't you want to marry my daddy? He's such a nice man. He'll take good care of you the same way he took care of Mama and me."

Isn't this dandy? First, I'm almost killed by a maniac. Next, I'm dumped by one of my boyfriends. And now, I have two ghosts strong-arming me into a quickie marriage to the other man in my life. Geesh. I can't catch a break.

I plastered a sincere-looking smile on my kisser and leaned over on my cane to get closer to the level of the ghost of Buddy's baby girl. "You're right, sweetie. Your daddy is a wonderful man and I care for him quite a bit. And maybe someday we will get married. *I hope you understand that if we do*, it will be when *we* think it's the right time for *us*, not when somebody else thinks it's the right time."

Marie smiled wickedly. "Listen up girlie—that's all well and good. But *you better understand this*: it's no use you fighting the *inevitable*. Time isn't on your side. Justine and me have a*n eternity* to wait around here until you and mah Cajun Boy tie the knot. So, rest assured we'll encourage you in our *special way* to goose the process along…*for however long it takes*."

Before I could explain to Marie LaValle in *vivid detail exactly where she could shove her wedding plans*, the two ghosts disappeared into thin air.

Queenie walked in and glanced around the empty

room. "Who were you talking to?"

Queenster, you wouldn't believe me if I told you.

A word about the author...

Born in the Big Apple, award-winning cozy mystery author Susie Black now calls sunny Southern California home. Like the protagonist in her Holly Swimsuit Mystery Series, Susie is a successful apparel sales executive. Susie began telling stories as soon as she learned to talk. Now she's telling all the stories from her garment industry experiences in humorous mysteries.

She reads, writes, and speaks Spanish, albeit with an accent that sounds like Mildred from Michigan went on a Mexican vacation and is trying to fit in with the locals. Since life without pizza and ice cream as her core food groups wouldn't be worth living, she's a dedicated walker to keep her girlish figure. A voracious reader, she's also an avid stamp collector. Susie lives with a highly intelligent man and has one incredibly brainy but smart-aleck adult son who inexplicably blames his sarcasm on an inherited genetic defect.

Looking for more? Visit her website: www.authorsusieblack.com Sign up for her reader list and receive a free swimwear fit guide. Or reach her at mysteries_@authorsusieblack.com